CARAVAN

The rowdies stopped again. The stakes were getting higher, and they were uncertain what to do. The leader was in the worst position — he didn't dare lose face in front of his buddies. So, after eyeing the switchblade for a moment, he calmly reached down to his belt and pulled his own weapon, an army surplus bayonet mounted on a wooden handle. "If you want to play games, we can do that too — right, fellas?" Inspired by his behavior, the others drew their knives.

Peter looked around. No one else in the park was in a position to see what was going on — or, if they were, they were doing a good job of ignoring it. He felt a queasy sensation in his stomach and the spit in his mouth tasted sour. He checked that his own knife was loose in its scabbard, should it be needed.

The pack was circling in on its prey, but with less confidence than it might ideally feel. The prospective victim was not some helpless stranger frightened by their bullying, but a powerful-looking man with a sharp knife and an apparent knowledge of how to use it. The gang moved in cautiously.

The black stood his ground, turning slowly to keep an eye on the people behind him as well as those in front. His knife hand stayed limber and pointed directly at the leader's throat.

THE FIRST TWELVE
LASER BOOKS

\# 1 . . . . **Renegades of Time**
by Raymond F. Jones

\# 2 . . . . **Herds**
by Stephen Goldin

\# 3 . . . . **Crash Landing On Iduna**
by Arthur Tofte

\# 4 . . . . **Gates of the Universe**
by R. Coulson and G. DeWeese

\# 5 . . . . **Walls Within Walls**
by Arthur Tofte

\# 6 . . . . **Serving in Time**
by Gordon Eklund

\# 7 . . . . **Seeklight**
by K. W. Jeter

\# 8 . . . . **Caravan**
by Stephen Goldin

\# 9 . . . . **Invasion**
by Aaron Wolfe

\#10 . . . . **Falling Toward Forever**
by Gordon Eklund

\#11 . . . . **Unto The Last Generation**
by Juanita Coulson

\#12 . . . . **The King of Eolim**
by Raymond F. Jones

STEPHEN GOLDIN

CARAVAN

COVER
ILLUSTRATION
BY
KELLY
FREAS

Laser Books

To Kathleen
My own reason for survival

CARAVAN

A LASER BOOK/first published 1975

ISBN 0-373-72008-4

Printed in U.S.A.

CHAPTER 1

WASHINGTON—International meetings on the economy opened here Monday with tones of gloom and distress over higher oil prices and the threat of world depression.

H. Johannes Witteveen, managing director of the International Monetary Fund, predicted continuing recession and inflation around the world, along with unprecedented financial strains.

World Bank President Robert S. McNamara forecast mass starvation in the world's poorest countries, containing populations totaling one billion, unless industrial and oil-exporting nations alike sharply step up their aid—a move few of these countries seem likely to make.

—*Los Angeles Times*
Tuesday October 1, 1974

We sit on the lip of a precipice, daring the force of gravity to pull us into the pit. The bottom is unfathomable because we've climbed so high we've lost sight of it. It is nothing so trivial as a recession; even a depression similar to the one in the

1930's would pale by comparison. What we are facing as we stare down into the abyss is nothing less than the total destruction of our present Civilization—and most of us, through a fear of heights, have shut our eyes. . . .

If you climb only a little way up a hillside and slip, you probably won't be hurt too much. Falls from greater heights can be fatal. We have climbed so high on the hillside of Progress that a fall will shatter us like a glass dropped from Mt. Everest....

—Peter Stone
World Collapse

*   *   *

The sign over the desk read "Granada Hills Security Checkpoint," but that did not disguise the fact that this building was actually a deserted supermarket at the edge of a deserted shopping center. Aisle upon aisle of denuded shelves gave mute testimony to the bad times that had befallen the community. In fact, the empty cavern of a building seemed to Peter to symbolize the entire Collapse of Civilization.

The guard behind the desk looked at him suspiciously. Peter didn't know much about guns, but the one in the guard's shoulder holster looked big enough to stop a herd of rampaging elephants. Peter coughed nervously and cleared his throat. "I . . . I'd like to join your community, if I could," he said. "I'm thirty-two and a good worker. I can do almost anything that needs to be done."

The guard's scowl was skeptical. "What did you say your name was?"

"Peter Smith," he lied. His own name, Stone, had acquired too many bad connotations in recent years and he never gave it out any more. He had trouble enough going unrecognized without advertising himself further.

"Smith, eh? Can anyone in Granada Hills vouch for you?"

"Uh, no, I just got in. I've been bicycling down from San Francisco these past few months, and this looked to be a good place to settle."

"How are things up there?"

"Bad," Peter said. "It's bad all along the coast. From what I've seen of it, your area looks about average."

The guard grunted. "I'm afraid, Mr. Smith, that we can't accept you here. We've got too many people already without adding strangers. There's plenty of willing hands to work but limited resources to keep them fed, if you know what I mean."

"Sure," Peter nodded. The story was all too familiar to him. "In that case, I was wondering if I might buy some food from you. I've got money. . . ."

"Granada Hills is on barter until the money situation settles down again. Unless you've got something to trade, you're out of luck. Got any bullets, batteries, candles, tools or copper wire?" Peter shook his head. "What about your bike? We can always use another bike."

"Sorry, I need it myself. Things aren't too safe for a man on foot; the bike gives me a slim edge, at least."

The other nodded. "Things are rough, all right. I never thought I'd see the day when this sort of thing would happen to us."

"Look, is there any place in this area that does take

cash?" The sun was sinking and Peter wanted to settle in somewhere before nightfall. He'd had too many scary experiences in the dark lately.

"You might try San Fernando; last I heard, they were still taking money. You'd better watch them, though—they've got a rowdy bunch over there."

"How do I get there?"

"You take this street over here, Balboa, and go north about a mile to San Fernando Mission Boulevard, then east a couple of miles. Can't miss it."

"Thanks." Peter started wheeling his bike out of the supermarket.

"Good luck," the guard called after him. "I wouldn't want to be a stoner now for all the gold in Fort Knox."

Peter wondered idly as he pedaled along whether there was still any gold left in Fort Knox. There probably was, he decided; gold was not worth stealing at the moment. People had more immediate needs, like food, water, gasoline and electricity. *Somewhere,* he thought, *the U.S. government may be trying valiantly to carry on as though nothing unusual were happening, guarding that gold and the wealth it supposedly represents like a virgin dinosaur guarding a nest of infertile eggs. And if they think about the Collapse at all, they probably blame it on me—as if I were anything but the messenger who brought the tidings of disaster.*

Being a prophet of doom is not a rewarding career.

As he pedaled up Balboa Boulevard, Peter looked around him and tried to imagine how the neighborhood must have looked ten years ago, before the Collapse really got underway. On his left was another

8

shopping center and a tall building that had once, according to a sign, been a hospital; currently it was being used as a series of apartments. On his right were more expressly designed apartments, once luxurious but now worn down and ugly. Rubbish that could not be burned had been dumped outside, lining the street and giving the air an unpleasant odor.

He passed another deserted supermarket as he crossed Chatsworth Street and continued north. There were houses on both sides of him, the ticky-tacky boxes that had been very popular in suburban communities at one time. They had little front yards that now contained gardens instead of lawns—lettuce, radishes, tomatoes and melons all seemed popular. The gardens were surrounded by fences—and some of the fencing, he noticed, had come from the center divider of a freeway. A stop sign had been stuck in one garden and dressed in tattered clothes to form a makeshift scarecrow. A couple of houses appeared to have been razed to make room for corn fields. The green stalks swayed proudly in the breeze.

Dogs roamed the streets and patrolled in front of the houses. They barked at him as he went past, but didn't bother to chase him when they saw he was no threat to their masters' gardens. There were several goats standing around and a large number of chickens, but Peter could see no cats running loose—they and rabbits would be penned up and used for food. Pets were no longer an affordable luxury. Birds, too, were scarce; no doubt the neighborhood children were improving their aim with slingshots.

Peter wondered what it was that made him hang around urban centers. The cities, he knew, were deathtraps, due to collapse of their own weight in the immediate future, and anyone caught in them would share in their destruction. It was the relatively small number of people living in the country who would fare the best, though they would be scarred as well. Any sensible person should see that and try to grab himself a piece of farmland before total havoc settled on the nation. But Peter was, and always had been, a city boy and was drawn to the cities even though he knew it might mean his death at any moment.

My problem, he decided, *is that I give good advice but, like everyone else, I refuse to follow it.*

Perhaps it had even been too late to do anything seven years earlier when his book, *World Collapse,* had hit the stands and fueled the controversy. Already the vast global forces he had foreseen were working to destroy Civilization. Shortages of materials had become noticeable as early as the 1970's, yet the series of small crises kept escalating without any serious steps being taken to prevent them. The divisiveness of society, with group pitted against group, had shorn humanity of the cohesion it needed to deal with its problems. Inflation had crippled the economy and strikes had weakened people's confidence in the predictable.

Many books had been written previously predicting that conditions would become critical before the end of the Twentieth Century; they had all been dismissed as doom-crying and overly pessimistic by the vast majority of people, who had retained a naive faith in the abilities of Mankind to rise, Phoenix-like, from its own excrement. Then *World Collapse* had come along, with the most forceful and frightening arguments to date. The then twenty-five year old Peter Stone proved beyond doubt that Civilization was doomed in just a couple of years unless radical steps were taken immediately. He even outlined what those steps were: mandatory euthanasia, mandatory birth control, immediate redistribution of wealth, immediate decentralization of society, an end to single family dwellings, an end to raising non-food animals as pets, forced movements of people to equalize population distribution, strict rationing of food and water, complete government takeover of industry and labor, complete government control of transportation, and a multi-billion-dollar crash program for farming and colonizing the sea beds.

It was, to him, amazing that he could antagonize ninety-five percent of the country virtually overnight. While a few intellectuals hailed him as "one of the greatest minds of our time," the nicest thing most people could find to call him was "that damned socialist." Some were convinced he was the devil incarnate for simply stating the obvious truth. But the book sold, millions of copies. It was ironic, Peter thought, that his book would be one of the last best-sellers; shortly after the book's twentieth printing, most of the printers' unions had gone out on strike. For all Peter knew they were still striking.

He had amassed fame and fortune when both commodities were fast losing their rewards. He had appeared on numerous television talk shows, explaining and debating his beliefs that Civilization, not just in the U.S. but around the world, was crumbling. He kept telling people that he didn't like his solutions, either, but that something drastic would have to be done to avoid an even worse fate. Nobody listened. His enemies called him an opportunist, making money off the world's misfortune, profiting on disaster. He was painted as a villain and branded a radical and a traitor.

In the meantime, everything he had predicted was coming true. Strikes by municipal workers brought about a breakdown of city services. The gasoline shortages he had foreseen were made even more acute by the final Israeli War, which devastated ninety-three per cent of the Arab oil fields. Overnight, the world faced its most severe energy crisis. Lacking power, radio and TV stations went off the air one by one. Lacking gasoline, truckers could no longer distribute materials, supplies and finished goods with their former efficiency. Everything was in short supply and getting shorter. Communication, transportation and distribution—the "Big Three" that Peter had listed in his book—were deteriorating with each passing day.

Peter turned right on San Fernando Mission Boulevard and continued riding. Telephone poles were spaced sporadically along the sides of the street; most had been chopped down for firewood. As he passed the houses he saw plenty of people working in their gardens. They would probably continue wrapping themselves in minutiae right up until the day the water stopped being pumped into their taps. Peter shuddered as he thought about the panic that was building under the surface, like a malevolent genie waiting for the inevitable day it would be set free.

He went under a freeway overpass, crossed a major street and finally came to an area that had once been a park. It was about three city blocks in length and one in width. An attempt had been made to grow corn here, too, but it was thwarted by the crowds that had moved in. The park was jammed with broken old cars that people had pushed there and were using as living quarters. At first, Peter wondered why they had bothered—housing was the least severe of the shortages at the moment. Then he saw what was across the street from the park.

It was the San Fernando Mission, one of the sanctuaries established in the Eighteenth Century by Father Junipero Serra along what came to be called El Camino Real. As a Catholic church, it represented one of the few organizations still operating in the world today. The mission was acting as a food distribution point, probably feeding the indigent as part of its charitable work. The charity was what had caused the swarms of poor people to move into the park across the street.

Peter had mixed feelings about the churches. Not being religious himself, he tended to distrust them. True, they were doing very good work now, providing not only temporal care—such as food distribution—but also tending to people's spiritual needs and keeping up morale. As the situation got progressively worse, people would turn increasingly to religion as a source of comfort. That was fine as far as it went, but Peter could not help recalling how the medieval Church had grown into a mind-numbing monolith, encouraging superstition and ruthlessly crushing all individuality. If Mankind were to rise and grow again, freedom of thought would be an absolute necessity. Peter was afraid the churches were bringing short-term relief and long-term oppression.

He stopped outside the mission and dismounted. This looked like his best prospect for spending the night. He could be fed at the mission and then sleep through the night sitting up against the wall. The nights could be chilly in Los Angeles but usually weren't unbearably cold. One of his few possessions —aside from money, which was only occasionally useful—was the blanket tucked in his knapsack. That would be enough to keep him warm tonight.

He started to walk his bike over to the mission when he noticed something going on down a side street just to the west of the building's wall. A black man with a motorcycle was being hassled by a pack of young whites.

"I think he's from Pacoima," one of the rowdies was saying. "Coming over here to spy on us, find out where our soft spots are. Probably him and his buddies want to make a gas raid tonight. Come on, shine, where'd you get that chopper?"

The black was young, tall and angular; in happier days, he might have been a college basketball player. He wore a red tanktop shirt, blue pants and a red bandana around his forehead. His face was adorned with a crisp black goatee and mustache, and was topped with a short mane of curly hair. He bore an expression of smoldering dignity. "You touch that cycle," he said, "and I'll carve the Gettysburg Address in your lily-white ass." His voice was so quiet as to be almost inaudible, yet carried a feel of power with it.

14

The pack was startled for a moment, then the fellows laughed nervously. They outnumbered the stranger nine to one. "Who do you think you are, nigger, coming around here and giving orders?" asked the leader, moving a step closer. The rest of the pack did the same.

In one swift motion, the stranger reached into his pants pocket, whipped out a switchblade and flipped the knife open. His hand moved in a little circle in front of him, giving the appearance that the blade was floating on its own. "Not orders," he said. "Just sound advice."

The rowdies stopped again. The stakes were getting higher, and they were uncertain what to do. The leader was in the worst position—he didn't dare lose face in front of his buddies. So, after eyeing the switchblade for a moment, he calmly reached down to his belt and pulled his own weapon, an army surplus bayonet mounted on a wooden handle. "If you want to play games, we can do that too—right, fellas?" Inspired by his behavior, the others drew their knives.

Peter looked around. No one else in the park was in a position to see what was going on—or, if they were, they were doing a good job of ignoring it. He felt a queasy sensation in his stomach and the spit in his mouth tasted sour. He checked that his own knife was loose in its scabbard, should it be needed.

The pack was circling in on its prey, but with less confidence than it might ideally feel. The prospective victim was not some helpless stranger frightened by their bullying, but a powerful-looking man with a sharp knife and an apparent knowledge of how to use it. The gang moved in cautiously.

The black stood his ground, turning slowly to keep an eye on the people behind him as well as those in front. His knife hand stayed limber and pointed directly at the leader's throat.

With a loud, bull-like bellow, the leader charged. The black sidestepped him easily and flicked his wrist in what seemed an effortless motion—yet, when the leader straightened up again, Peter could see that a deep slash had been cut across his left ear and was bleeding profusely. "Next," said the black, laughing.

Three others came charging from different directions. One received a quick kick to the groin that doubled him up in a hurry; the second found himself stabbing air as the victim had whirled away and brought a slashing blow down on the hand of the third. "Come on," yelled the gang's leader from the sidelines. "What are we, a bunch of chickens? Let's get him!"

They all converged at once, though showing a great respect for their victim's prowess. The black had a longer reach than most of them and was able to keep them momentarily at bay with his slashes, but he couldn't last forever against their superior numbers.

Peter was not a very good fighter, though he'd had more than his share of practice over the last year. He usually avoided fights if he could, but this was one he couldn't ignore if he wanted to live with his conscience. Drawing his knife and emitting a loud whoop, he rushed forward.

The gang was startled by this attack from a new direction and froze momentarily, giving Peter an advantage he badly needed. He incapacitated one of the foe with a quick stab to the side, under the ribs. Turning to the next man, he lashed out across the face, cutting just above the eyebrow. Blood streamed out of the cut and into the eye, blinding the fellow and making him think his eye had been put out. He dropped to the ground, screaming.

The black had not hesitated when the attackers did. His knife was busy slashing away at his opponents, making them put up their guard and fight defensively. But now they had recovered from the surprise of Peter's attack, and were launching a counter-offensive of their own. Peter found himself facing two big menacing types with murder in their eyes. Without the element of surprise on his side, the other two were undoubtedly the better fighters. Peter backed slowly away from them until he found that his back was right up against the wall of the mission. The other two kept closing on him, evil grins on their faces.

The one on his left lunged at him. Peter tried to twist away, but wasn't quick enough—the attacker's knife cut across the top of his left arm, sending a shot of pain through Peter's body. Blood poured out, staining his already grubby shirt, but he had little time for worrying about that—he was fighting for his life.

His twisting had put him in a bad position, because now he had his left side outward and his right side—along with his knife hand—towards the wall. He had to duck rapidly as the second attacker, seeing the opening, made a vicious swipe at his head. The blade whistled barely a quarter of an inch over Peter's hair.

In making that slash, though, the youth had left himself open. Peter charged forward and thrust his knife into the attacker's gut. The man let out a cry of pain and crumpled slowly to the ground. Peter pulled his blade out quickly, fell to the ground and rolled to get away from the first attacker, who was coming at him again.

When he got to his feet, he saw the man facing him in a low crouched stance. They circled one another for a long second, then the fellow charged. Peter tried to play matador, sidestepping the charge and parrying the thrust, but he was only partially successful. The other's knife cut through his shirt and scratched the ribs on his left side. Peter turned and backed away again.

The other, sensing a quick kill, charged again. He got only halfway to Peter, though, before he screamed and fell forward. A switchblade was embedded in his neck.

Peter looked around, surveying the battlefield. Seven bodies were scattered around the ground, most of them alive but severely wounded. The remaining two gang members were fleeing down the street. In the middle of most of the devastation, the black man calmly admired his handiwork. He appeared unscathed. With a grin at Peter he walked over and pulled his switchblade out of the throat of his last victim, wiped it off on the man's shirt, folded it up and stuck it back in his pocket. Then he walked over to his motorcycle, prepared to drive off.

"Hey," said Peter, "aren't you even going to thank me?"

The other turned. "Thank you? For what? Doin' something that anybody with any guts should've done?"

"But it wasn't anybody, it was *me,* and I'm bleeding."

The black ambled over, grabbed Peter's wounded left arm roughly and examined it. "Sheeyit, man, that ain't nothing but a flesh wound. It'll heal up, 'less it gets infected." He stopped as an idea occurred to him. "You live around here?"

Peter shook his head.

"Oh, a stoner, huh?" Peter hated that expression. Since the Collapse had begun, a lot of people had left their homes and taken to roaming, looking for someplace better than the one they'd left. Supposedly the term "stoner" had come about because these people were described as "rolling stones," but Peter had more than a little suspicion that the word was also a play on his name.

"Look," the man continued, "how'd you like to settle down somewhere that's peaceful, where there ain't no shortages and everybody works together?"

Peter eyed him warily. "Sure, who wouldn't? Only where are you going to find a place like that? Your back yard?"

"Don't get cute, man, I asked a legit question."

"And I said yes."

"What's your name?"

"Peter Smith." The lying came by reflex now.

The black extended his hand. "Kudjo Wilson." They slapped palms instead of shaking. "Listen, if

19

you really want to go on to somethin' better than all this," and he waved his hand to include the park crammed with junked autos, "I think you'd better have a talk with my man."

Peter shrugged. "It can't hurt, I suppose. Where is he?"

"Oh, he's a few miles away yet. If you want, you can hop on the back and hold on, and I'll take you to him right away."

Peter shook his head. "Sorry, but I've got a bike that I'd rather not leave behind—and we can't really take it with us on that cycle."

"Right you are." The other thought for a minute. "Tell you what I'll do. I'll ride on ahead and tell him about you. He's going to be coming through here anyway, or damn close. Why don't you wait up alongside the freeway, the one over there." He pointed further east. "It's a couple of blocks that way. You wait just before the bridge of the overpass, southbound side. Do you have a watch?"

Peter shook his head again. "It was stolen a month and a half ago."

"Well, anyway, he'll be along in a couple of hours. It'll be after dark, if that doesn't bother you."

"Well. . . ." Peter began.

"Be there," the other advised. He started his motorcycle. "We won't wait." And he drove off.

Holding his sore left arm, Peter went back to his bicycle. After the fight with those toughs the mission might not be the best place for him to spend the night, after all—they might come back with friends, looking for revenge. His stomach was rumbling from not having been fed since breakfast, but it would be better to stay alive than to try for a free handout here and later be murdered in his sleep.

He pedaled further east along San Fernando Mission Boulevard and eventually came to the overpass that Kudjo Wilson had mentioned. The sun had just set and the sky was getting ominously dark. He paused at the bridge and looked up at it. Should he believe what the black had said? He had long ago given up believing in fairy tales, and that story had sounded suspiciously like a modern-day El Dorado. A place of peace and plenty would be very hard to come by, and invitations to it just wouldn't pop into his lap so casually. Besides, how could a black man hold the key to Utopia? It didn't make sense. If there were such a place, what was that Kudjo Wilson doing *here?*

But then again, what did he have to lose? If this were an ambush, what could they take from him besides his bicycle, a blanket and some practically worthless money? It would be little enough loot for such an elaborately planned trap. Besides, Wilson could have robbed him of all that right on the spot if he'd wanted to. The whole affair was very puzzling.

Peter wheeled his bike up the on ramp and parked it by the side of the bridge.

He sat there in the dark, waiting. Traffic on the freeway was virtually nonexistent due to the lack of gasoline—only two cars in over an hour's time, and they whizzed by him in the fast lane without even slowing. He wondered whether the people he wanted had passed him by without even seeing him, or whether they would ever come at all. This whole thing could be an elaborate and incomprehensible practical joke.

You're a fool, he told himself sternly. *Listening to stories of Never-Never Land at your age. You'd probably buy the Golden Gate Bridge if someone offered it to you right now.* But he stayed, because there was nowhere else to go.

After what must have been another hour, he saw some headlights approaching from the north. These were traveling much slower than the cars that whizzed past, and as they came closer Peter could make out a whole string of cars in a procession. The leading vehicle stopped just before getting to the bridge and pulled off to the side of the road. The cars behind it followed its example.

A spotlight stabbed out at him from the top of the vehicle, blinding him with its glare. "Mr. Smith?" called out a strange voice.

"Yes," he answered.

"Come on in, we've been hoping you'd be here. Would you like some dinner?"

CHAPTER 2

"First-Class mail service is now the worst in memory," contends the Wall Street Journal. An example of the problem occurred last month when a bag of mail disappeared in Prince George's County, Md., causing headaches for a number of residents. Mrs. Ernest Drumheller, who lives in Clinton, Md., says she returned from a vacation to find that her telephone had been disconnected because her check for her bill hadn't reached the phone company. It cost her $10 to get the service reinstated. Several customers of the People's National Bank in Clinton stopped payments on checks that they feared were in the missing bag. . . .

—*Los Angeles Times*
Wednesday September 11, 1974

Communication is one of the Big Three of any civilization. People and organizations can only interact to the extent that they can communicate with one another. Little or no communication means suspicion, hatred and conflict. As communications increase and improve the foreign becomes less fearful, and peaceful interaction becomes feasible. . . .

In the time of the Greeks the manageable political unit was the city-state, and its size was determined by how far a man could walk in a day. This ensured that everyone would be no more than one day out of touch with current events. Neighboring city-states, with whom communication was far less frequent and far more out-of-date, were treated with distrust. . . .

Communications today are practically instantaneous anywhere on the globe. That fact has enabled us to develop a global civilization. But, in building this network so quickly, we may have stretched ourselves too far. Like a rubber band extended past its breaking point, the snap backwards will be sharp and painful. . . .

—Peter Stone
World Collapse

*　　*　　*

As Peter approached the first vehicle, he was startled to see that it was an armored truck, the type that used to carry money to banks and stores. It sat squat and ominous, its square gray shape impassive before him. The spotlight from its roof stung his eyes, which were accustomed to the darkness, but he could make out that the second vehicle in the train was also armored. The rest of the cars behind it were just dim shapes in shadows; Peter could not tell how many there were or what they looked like.

A lean figure got out of the second truck and came

over to meet him at the door of the first. It was Kudjo Wilson. "Glad you could make it," he said, opening the door on the passenger side of the truck's cab. "Let me make the introductions."

He stuck his head inside the cab. "Honon, this is my man Peter. Peter, may I present to you the honorable, the distinguished, the inestimable Israel Baumberg."

There was a small battery-powered lantern glowing inside the cab, and it cast sufficient light for Peter to make out the man he was being introduced to. Even seated, Israel Baumberg was a big man, with broad shoulders and powerful arms. Standing, he must easily have been six foot three or four. His hair was straight and black, cut short in almost a bowl haircut. His face was lined and weathered, looking more like finely tanned leather than flesh. It was hard to distinguished skin tones in the feeble light, but from the structure of the features Peter would have guessed that this man was dark-complected. An automatic rifle and a machine gun were propped casually beside him.

"Welcome to our caravan, Mr. Smith. Come on in." As Peter entered, the other peered at him through the faint glow. "Or should I say Mr. Stone? This is an unexpected honor."

Peter grimaced. The recognition was unwelcome; too many people harbored bad feelings toward him. But he climbed into the cab and sat in the passenger's seat.

"Let me see your arm," the big man continued. "Kudjo told me you'd hurt it." He examined the wound tenderly. "Well, it doesn't look too bad, but we don't want any nasty surprises along the way so we'd better have it tended to. Kudjo, could you go back and see if Sarah's free? And while you're at it, check on how they're coming with dinner."

"Yassa, Boss," Kudjo grinned in a parody of the old-time subservient blacks. He moved down the line of cars to carry out instructions.

"Good man, that Kudjo. You were lucky to run into him. He used to be an undercover narcotics officer for the St. Louis police. They don't make them any better. As for myself, before you start asking questions, my father was Jewish and my mother was an Indian, and I prefer to go by my Indian name, Honon, which means 'bear.' That's enough about me for the moment. Any questions?"

"Yes—what's this all about?"

"This," Honon spread his hands to include the entourage behind his truck, "is a caravan that Kudjo and I are leading. We are in the process of going from here to there."

"I know where here is, but what's 'there'?"

"That's a long story, which I'll begin in just a minute. We started in San Francisco this time, and have been working our way down the California coast. You're very lucky to have met us; we were coming down route 101 and would have missed this area completely, except that an earthquake wrecked the road just south of Ventura. We had to backtrack up to 138 and across Santa Paula to Interstate 5, which is where we are right now. We'll probably camp here for the night and move on tomorrow."

At this point a woman stuck her head through the

open doorway of the passenger side. She looked to be in her forties, with gray-blonde hair and a slightly chubby face. "I hear you've got someone who needs looking at," she said to Honon.

"Right. Peter, this is Dr. Sarah Finkelstein, who will be ministering to our ills this trip. Sarah, I'd like you to meet the notorious Peter Stone."

Peter winced again at the introduction. The doctor looked him up and down critically. "Well, well, well. The Man Who Turned Out To Be Right. Is it any consolation?"

"It never was."

"I suppose not. Well, let's see what you've got." She examined his wound, clucking silently to herself. "Is your tetanus shot current?" she asked.

"Haven't had one in years."

"It was a silly question, I know, but old habits die hard. You won't be getting one from me, either; I'm out of vaccine. It doesn't look too bad, though. I'll clean it and bandage it for you. You'll be a bit stiff, but you'll survive. As to my next question, it'll sound a little personal but it's necessary. Do you have any venereal disease?"

Peter was startled at her bluntness, but answered no. "Good," she said. "We must try to keep our breeding stock pure." Without further elaboration, she went to work on his arm quietly and efficiently, then left Peter and Honon alone.

"Before I begin my full story," Honon said, "there are a couple of facts needed as preludes. You are familiar, no doubt, with the advances in the field of cryogenics and suspended animation."

Peter nodded. "I mentioned them in my book."

27

"Yes, that's right. Excuse me, I had forgotten—it's been a while since I've had the time to reread it. As I recall, you didn't have anything complimentary to say about them."

"They were a wasted effort, a futile grabbing for immortality. What possible advantage could there be in freezing someone to be awakened fifty years from now, when all indications were that the world at that time would have difficulty supporting even the few people it would have left? People from the past would be totally helpless in a new world wracked by famine, drought, war and plague. The money and talent that went into that research could have been used better elsewhere."

"Perhaps," Honon said, "but there might have been some ramifications that even you did not foresee."

"Such as?"

"Not so fast. Have you ever heard of a star called Epsilon Eridani?"

"I'm afraid astronomy was never my field."

"Nor mine. But fortunately there were a few people who took an interest in it. A couple years back, before the space program disintegrated completely, they conducted an experiment in what they called satellite parallax—don't ask me to explain it, I can't—and they found that Epsilon Eridani had a whole series of planets, just like our own sun. It was an interesting find, but the world had more pressing problems and paid it little notice.

"At about that same time, a man wrote a book. It was a big book, a powerful book, and it scared a lot of people. It talked about an end to Civilization and a return to barbarism because of overpopulation, depletion of raw materials and a general breakdown of cohesive forces. Most people became angry at this because it was a fact that they were afraid to face. . . ."

"You're telling me," Peter muttered.

". . . But a few people actually became thoughtful. The author's contentions were unarguable, but these thoughtful people still did not want to see the end of Civilization. So they began thinking of alternatives."

"So did I, and I was hated for it. Sure, my suggestions were radical, but I was dealing with a crisis situation. My plans might not have worked, but they couldn't have been any worse than the hell we're going through now."

Honon shrugged. "Who's to say? At any rate, these thoughtful people saw the resentment aimed at you and decided to do their own work secretly. They included some people with a lot of influence, some with a lot of money, and a few with both."

"That always helps."

"So they built their starship . . . ."

Peter gasped. "Hey, wait a minute. I think I missed a step in there. What's this about a starship?"

"Think about it; use that incisive mind of yours. If the Earth is used up, then Civilization would stand a better chance elsewhere if it's to continue and grow, correct? Where else is there? Certainly no other planet in our solar system is capable of housing a colony without an enormous technology to back it up. So that leaves us the stars—in particular, Epsilon Eridani."

Peter was about to say something when a little girl

knocked on the door of the truck. She was dark-haired, and couldn't have been more than eight or nine years old. "Mister Honon," she said, "I've got some dinner for you and the other man."

"Thanks, Mary." Honon reached out his window and grabbed two bowls from her. "Careful," he said to Peter as he handed one of them over. "They're hot." The little girl left to go back where she had come from.

The liquid in the bowls was of a consistency half-way between soup and stew. It had potatoes, peas, beans, carrots, soybeans and even small pieces of chicken—practically a smorgasbord by today's standards. Peter's stomach was screaming to him that he hadn't had anything to eat since a very skimpy breakfast this morning. He accepted the spoon that Honon proffered and put some of the mixture in his mouth, savoring the combination of tastes. "You eat pretty well," he said.

"Thank you. As I mentioned, we're trying to keep Civilization alive, and one of its more enjoyable aspects is good food. We do what we can while we're traveling, but even this is far from a balanced meal."

"There are people who would kill for some of this."

Honon sighed. "Yes, I know there are. They've made a couple of attempts already, which is why we prefer to use armored vehicles to lead this procession. Traveling these days is not something you do on a whim."

Both men ate silently for awhile, realizing that their meal was literally a treasure in this depleted world. Peter finished first and leaned back contentedly.

"Thank you very much. That was the best food I've had in weeks."

"Would you like some more? I could send back for a refill."

"I don't want to make inroads on your supplies...."

"We'll be okay for awhile. The whole back of that second truck is crammed with freeze-dried stuff."

Peter was sorely tempted but decided to refrain. "I don't want to get too used to rich living," he said. "Situations can change so abruptly."

Honon nodded. "That's true, but it doesn't stop me from living well when I can. I learned when I was riding herd that you survive the bad times and live it up in the good times."

"You were a cattleman, then?"

"I've been pretty much of everything, at one time or another. Lumberjack, truck driver, forest ranger, farm hand, carpenter, dishwasher—I like doing something new all the time."

"And now you're a wagonmaster."

"Yep. You see, the way I figure it, you've always got to be moving toward something. Traveling isn't enough; you've got to have a goal in mind."

"And your goal is the stars?"

"Not immediately. First I have to get this party to the Monastery."

"The what?"

"That's what we call our little colony. Since it was the monasteries that kept knowledge alive during the first Dark Ages, we thought we'd name our base after them. It has no religious significance, I assure you; we're all pretty tolerant. It's hard enough surviving today without reviving old prejudices."

31

"That doesn't stop most people. Bigotry seems to have reached a high point," Peter said bitterly.

Honon shrugged. "I don't really care if they kill themselves off. The way I see it, the race can only be improved by the removal of bigots from the gene pool."

"Where is this Monastery of yours?"

"Oh, it's out there somewhere." Honon waved his hand in a general easterly direction. "I can't be more specific, I'm afraid. It *is* secret, and with good reason. We live too well to suit most people on the outside. If they knew where we were, they'd come and tear us down. That's why I can't tell the people in the caravan exactly where we're going—in case they drop out or get separated from us, they won't be able to tell anyone else."

"But if your planning an interstellar colony, you must have an awful lot of people. . . ."

"Nearly five thousand, at last count."

Peter whistled. "But it's impossible to hide that many people."

"We manage," Honon smiled.

"But getting that many people off Earth would be a major problem in itself. How do you propose to do it?"

"For one thing, not everyone is going. Some of us have a sentimental attachment to this old world, and we'd like to stick around and rehabilitate it if we can. Only about three thousand will be making the trip."

"But even so, the fuel requirements. . . ."

"In the last year or so of the space program a development slipped right past the press, who were busy covering wars, shortages and the like: nuclear propulsion, which lets you lift large payloads with small outlay. It's unproven in manned flight, but ground experiments are very promising."

"I don't pretend to be an astronautical engineer, but I do remember seeing a planetarium show once that said that it would take thousands of years to get from here to even the nearest star. You can't expect the colonists to live that long—and the food alone for three thousand people would fill several ships."

"Those quickie figures, I'm told, were based on constant velocity. What the nuclear drive gives us, instead, is constant acceleration—one ten-thousandth of a 'gee,' to be precise. I know that doesn't sound like much, but it adds up. The latest estimates are that you can make the trip in only six hundred and fifty years."

"But even so. . . ."

"Remember what I was saying earlier about the coldsleep techniques? Colonists will be frozen just before takeoff and, except for the ship's crew, won't wake up until they've landed on their new home. It will save on supplies and on room, since we won't have to allow space for that many people to be walking around."

Peter sat still for a moment, thinking and considering the possibilities. "You're either crazy," he said at last, "or the most hopeless dreamer I know."

"A little of both, I hope. We're living in a very sane, very dreamless age, and look at the mess it's in. There is nothing more sane than trying to stay alive, which is what everybody out there is struggling to do. For them, it's a full-time business. They have no time for dreams. As a result, they're living lives of borderline survival, and it's getting worse. As for me, I insist on looking up at the sky every so often and wondering whether things could be better. Fantasy may be slightly insane, but no intelligent creature can last long without it.

"Besides," he added, pointing an accusing finger at Peter, "you're a fine one to criticize. Don't think I can't see behind that mask of the cynic you wear like a Greek tragedian. Mark Twain, when accused of being a pessimist in his old age, remarked rather that he was 'an optimist who did not arrive.' If you did not idealize, if you did not see the world as it should be, you never could have packed into your book all the fire and anger you felt."

"Really?" Peter asked, raising an amused eyebrow. Many people had tried to psychoanalyze him through his book, with varied success.

"A cynic is just a frustrated optimist. You have to have ideals in the first place to be disappointed that they aren't achieved. You, Peter Stone, are a builder of utopias without a good supply of timber.

"And that's why you want me to come along—because I'm a failure here and you want to give me another chance? Excuse me for being a cynic, but I don't believe that."

Honon shook his head. "Not at all. I want to give Humanity another chance, and I think you could be of help. You think about social phenomena. You see the alternatives where other people are blind, and you're not afraid to talk about them openly. We'll need a good alternatives spotter and social critic if we're going to make it. There you have it— the ground rules and the job description. I'll need

34

an answer, a commitment from you *now*, because I won't be back this way again. Do you want the job?"

Peter didn't even hesitate. "Well, the pay's lousy but the fringe benefits seem okay. If you cut me off a piece of that dream, I think I can swallow it."

CHAPTER 3

Billions of dollars have been spent in recent years to improve law enforcement—yet crime has continued to rise, and many Americans are worried about whether it can ever be brought under control. . . .

Patrick V. Murphy, a former police official in Washington and New York . . . says this: "We have to face facts. There is too much instability in our cities. As long as we have unemployment, underemployment, broken homes, alcoholism, drugs and mental-health problems, we are going to have crime."

—*U.S. News & World Report*
June 10, 1974

Crime is an outlet many people have for coping with a society whose complexities have outgrown their bounds. In its last attempt to hold itself together, I predict our culture will go through one last monstrous spasm of "law and order." Everything different from the norm will be subjected to the severest kinds of repression in society's desperate efforts to keep afloat.

The real tragedy of this, though, is the aftereffects the policy will have on post-Collapse society. The repression instilled now will linger on, like a frog's leg continuing to kick long after the body is dead. . . .

—Peter Stone
World Collapse

*　　*　　*

Peter spent the night in the cab of the armored truck with Honon. They talked for a while longer, comparing the experiences each had had in his travels around the country. Peter discovered that Honon had been traversing the nation regularly for the past four years, conducting these caravans. The picture he painted was not a cheery one. Hardship, starvation and strife were ubiquitous throughout the United States. Plague had not yet begun to take its toll, but conditions in the cities were building to the point where sanitation must break down and disease would begin to spread.

"In some ways," Honon said, "it's fortunate that the Collapse is worldwide. If the Jewish guerrillas hadn't started their urban warfare in Russia five years ago, the Russians might have taken advantage of our weakness and invaded. But with the Jews inside, the Chinese on their border and a dwindling supply of resources, they're in even worse shape than we are."

After a while the ache in Peter's arm and the exhaustion from the day's activities took their toll. He leaned back in the padded leather seat and got the first good night's sleep he'd had in days.

Honon woke him shortly after sunrise by shaking his good shoulder. "Rise and shine," he said cheerfully. "It's time for breakfast—and time, too, to meet the rest of the people you'll be sharing this trip with."

Peter climbed out of the cab and got his first good look at the full caravan. The first two vehicles in it were armored trucks—and after the picture Honon had painted of conditions around the country, Peter agreed that the caravan would have to be prepared for anything. Next in line was a large camper, alongside which a large group of people had gathered. Behind the camper was a blue and white Volkswagen van, and behind that were three more cars, all compact size. *It must make for an interesting parade,* Peter mused.

As Honon led him up to the camper, Peter could feel the gaze of the caravan members. They would have heard, by this time, of their notorious new companion. He wondered how many of them were already hating him.

"Everybody, gather 'round," Honon called, and the private conversations ceased. "I'd like you to meet our latest acquisition, Peter Stone. We all owe him a large debt of gratitude, I think, because it was his book that spurred our people to action. Without him, there might be no Monastery and no plans for the starship. Don't neglect to show him how grateful we are."

Peter was surprised at that introduction, and was even more surprised when the people responded as Honon had asked. They hung back hesitantly at first,

38

unsure of themselves, but then came forward in small groups to say hello and welcome him to their caravan. Men and women came over to shake his hand, and children smiled bashfully up at him.

"Sorry I can't stick around and introduce you to everybody," Honon said. "I've got to grab a quick breakfast and go out to see if I can recruit us a shoemaker."

"A shoemaker?"

"Yes, a good man who was recommended by someone in the Monastery. He lives down in central L.A." He saw the puzzlement on Peter's face and explained further. "Look, I suppose if you were manning a colony you'd pick all the smartest, most intellectual folks you could find. But I'll tell you right now, it wouldn't work. Some eggheads—even a lot of eggheads—are needed, sure, but you can't build a world out of doctors and nuclear physicists. The first time the plumbing failed, they'd be in big trouble. I have to recruit people who would be useful in a frontier situation. People who are already trained to produce what will be needed. You won't have factories where you're going, turning out assembly-line clothes for you; you'll need craftsmen who can make good shoes from scratch. The people on this trip are a hodge-podge, sure; but we're trying to save Humanity, and Humanity itself is a hodge-podge. Think about it."

Honon stepped up into the camper and after a moment emerged with a canteen, two big handfuls of wheatcakes and some dried fruit. "I'll see you a little later," he told Peter. "In the meantime, get to know everybody. I think you'll find they're a pretty good group." He went off to the first armored truck, took a motorcycle out of the back and rode off into town.

As Peter waited in line with the rest of the group for breakfast, members came up and introduced themselves. He met Dominic and Gina Gianelli of Oakland, a couple in their mid-thirties. Dom, as the man preferred to be called, was a carpenter "and a football fan. But it don't look like there'll be too many more football games for awhile." Peter could only agree. The Gianellis had five children, ranging in age from two to ten; though he was introduced to all of them he had trouble keeping them straight in his mind except for Mary, the eight year old who had delivered the food to Honon and him the night before.

He met Bill and Patty Lavochek from San Luis Obispo. The Lavocheks, both in their mid-twenties, had been married only four months, and were looking on this whole affair as an exciting adventure and a good way to start a new life. Bill, a machinist, was sure his talents would be greatly in demand at the Monastery and on the new world.

Peter also met Harvey and Willa Parks. Harv, a plumbing contractor from San Francisco, was a small, hard-bitten man in his late thirties. He had a brusque manner but a genuinely friendly disposition. Willa was about ten years younger than he was, a quiet, mousey woman who did what she was told efficiently and without complaint. They had two children, a girl, seven, and a boy, four.

Just before Peter reached the head of the line the

doctor, Sarah Finkelstein, came over to ask him how his arm was. He told her it was stiff but usable, and she asked him to let her know if any further problems developed.

At the front of the line, doing the serving, was a Japanese couple, Charlie and Helen Itsobu, both in their early thirties. Charlie had been assigned the cooking chores because he was a professional chef-chief cook, in fact, at what had been Peter's favorite Japanese restaurant in San Francisco. Peter realized how talented Charlie must be—a man that young didn't often rise that high in culinary circles—and complimented him. Charlie smiled and apologized that the fare was not as elegant as he preferred. He slipped Peter an extra wheatcake and winked at him.

As Peter walked away from the camper, the Gianellis waved at him, beckoning him to sit with them and share his mealtime. Peter did so gladly; it had been much too long since he'd had such companionship and he was getting drunk on the camaraderie. Kudjo slapped him on the back as he sat down, exchanged pleasantries, then got a second motorcycle out of the lead truck and drove off. "Where's he going?" Peter asked.

"Oh, he's our scout," Dom Gianelli told him. "He drives on head, looks things over, makes sure the route's safe. That's what he was doing yesterday when he found you."

Peter nodded. "That makes sense."

"He's a good man, that Kudjo. Would've made a cracking good football player, I'll bet. A natural wide receiver, by the looks of him."

"Mind if I join you people?" came a female voice from behind. "I can't pass up such a sterling opportunity to meet an eligible bachelor."

"Help yourself," Gina Gianelli smiled.

The girl who sat down beside Peter was short and somewhat squat, with stringy brown hair and large puppy eyes. Her most prominent feature, though, was her nose, which dominated her face and threatened to take over completely. "I'm Marcia Konigsburg, twenty-four and unmarried. Not that I'm measuring you for a wedding cake, but I think it's good to get these things out in the open at once. I design clothes for boutiques, and I also do some theater costumes. I suppose that's why Honon asked me to come along—wherever we end up, we'll need someone who can make the right clothes for the occasion."

Peter liked her instantly. She was a friendly, clinging sort whose amiable charm overcame the initial impression of homeliness. "I read your book, you know," she went on.

"So you're the one."

"Hey, you're funny, too. Yeah, it really impressed me. I was a sophomore in college then, and I guess just about everything impressed me. David Hume, Aleister Crowley and you were my three favorites."

"We certainly make an odd trio."

"If it's any consolation, my friends all told me I had no taste. That's the kind of people I run around with—crazy, all of them."

Peter suddenly felt a strange sensation on the back of his neck, as though he were being watched. Turning, he caught sight of a girl watching him from beside one of the cars. She was young, slender and blonde, with a look of almost angelic innocence. As he turned to look at her, though, she stared off in another direction, pretending not to notice. He shrugged his shoulders and turned back to the conversation.

Marcia had not even noticed his inattention and was running on to some extent about the breakdown of formal education, which she herself had witnessed. ". . . And it was just like you said—the classes had less and less to do with reality, not because they weren't trying to be relevant, but because reality was moving out from under them." Her wording was taken almost verbatim from his book; she must have committed it to memory.

Dom Gianelli waved at a tall man in a white knit shirt and black pants. "Father Tagon," he called, "why not come over and join us?"

The man so addressed followed the suggestion. "Wait 'til you meet this guy," Dom said to Peter. "He'll really be able to give you some arguments."

The newcomer was a tall, thin man in his late thirties, with a hawklike nose, brown eyes and a high forehead that gradually blended into a head of thinning brown hair. "Hi," he said, bending down towards Peter and proffering a hand. "I'm Jason Tagon."

"Did I hear Dom call you 'Father'?"

"He might also have called me 'Doctor'—I have a PhD. in astronomy. But yes, I am a priest. Titles don't seem to mean too much these days, and I prefer to be called Jason."

Peter nodded and stored that fact in his memory

file, which was rapidly becoming overloaded from this barrage of new names and faces. "Dom also said something about your giving me arguments."

"He worded that a little strongly. I can't argue with your predictions—they've obviously come true. It's your attitudes that bother me."

"About the Catholic Church?"

Jason smiled. "That is a small part of it. You did say—let me see if I can quote it—'the Catholic Church has done more than any other single organization in history to retard the course of human progress.'"

"I hope you didn't take that too personally; the fact is that the Catholic Church has been *around* longer than any other single organization in history. All organizations eventually become repressive to some extent—they pass a certain point in their existence where their function switches over to self-preservation rather than the administration of their original duty. I was speaking against the bureaucratic structure, not against individual Catholics."

"I realized that. But we individual Catholics are brought up to believe that the Church can do no wrong, and being slapped down for that still stings. But that wasn't my entire objection. As an ordained spokesman of God, I couldn't help but feel that you left Him out of your calculations."

"As an ordained agnostic," Peter countered, "I couldn't help but feel that the supernatural was a superfluous variable in my calculations. I was dealing primarily with social ecology. The rules were laid down by God—if indeed He exists—a long time ago, and I couldn't foresee any changes in the

ground rules once the game had started. I dealt exclusively with human beings."

"And you ignored the possibility of divine intervention."

"Let's say I would have welcomed it but was not
counting on it."

"What about this interstellar colonization attempt?"

"If you're trying to claim it's divine intervention,
I won't be able to disprove it. By the same token,
I defy you to prove that it isn't merely the work of
some dedicated, ingenious men."

"Touché," Jason smiled.

That same feeling of being watched hit Peter a
second time. He looked around and noticed the
blonde girl staring at him again from a few yards
away. "Who is she?" he asked the people around
him.

"That's Risa Svenson," Marcia volunteered. "We
picked her up in Monterey. Really strange sort of
girl, if you ask me."

"Strange? In what way?"

"Basically she's just shy," the priest explained.
"That and her youth tend to keep her a little apart
from the rest of us. She's really a nice person."

"I'd like to go over and talk to her for a bit.
Thank you all for sharing your breakfast time with
me. Jason, I'll be interested in continuing our discussion a little bit later."

He got up and walked over to the young girl,
who was again pretending not to notice him. "Excuse me for asking, but why were you staring at
me?"

She looked up at him, startled. "I wasn't. . . ."

"Yes you were. It doesn't bother me too much, but I would like to know why."

She opened her mouth to make an excuse, closed it, then said, "You were just so famous and all that I wanted to have a look at you. Is there something so wrong in that?"

"No. In fact, I'm rather relieved to discover that I don't look like the hideous monster you thought I'd be."

From the expression on her face, Peter knew he'd guessed her mood correctly. "I didn't really think you were a monster," she said hurriedly.

"Of course not."

"But I did hear so many bad things about you. . . ."

"Did you ever read my book?"

"No, I was a little too young. I saw the TV show about it, though. I didn't like it—it seemed so depressing and negative."

"It *was* depressing and negative, and I didn't like it either. But what can you do about the truth? If you just bury it in a corner, it digs its way out, comes over to you and bites you on the ankle."

"It all . . . I don't know. I want to feel there's some hope, somewhere, for the world. Your book left people feeling there was none."

"The situation was there for anyone to see. I happened to be the one to turn on the lights. It didn't help—people just closed their eyes and tripped over the future anyway. I only reported the facts."

"Facts aren't enough," the girl said. "We need dreams, too."

"How old are you?"

46

The girl looked at him defensively. "Nineteen, why?"

"When I was nineteen I had just gotten my Bachelor's degree in sociology. People were considering me some sort of genius and I went through an accelerated college program. I had dreams then, good ones. I was going to correct all the problems of the world, straighten things out so that we could live in peace." He shrugged his shoulders. "Then something happened—maybe I just grew up, I don't know. But in only a couple of years, all the dreams had turned to nightmares. The world was going merrily down the path to Hell, and no one was doing a damned thing to stop it. I tried to yell, I tried to put on the brakes, and people ignored me. Is it any wonder I felt hopeless?" He discovered, much to his chagrin, that there were tears in his eyes. *That's all I need, to break down and cry in front of this total stranger,* he thought, at the same time wondering why she should affect him so strongly that he had to cry.

But to his surprise the girl's attitude softened at once. "I'm sorry," she said, reaching out gently to touch his arm. "I didn't know. That sounds so sad, having all your hopes die like that."

"Scratch any cynic and you'll find an optimist who's been disillusioned."

"Poor baby," she said, gazing at him with enormous blue eyes. "Would you care to talk about it?"

They sat down on the freeway embankment beside the caravan, and before he realized it Peter found himself telling this strange, beautiful girl the story of his life.

Honon returned a couple hours after noon. "No luck there," he told the people, and explained privately to Peter, "You can understand how it is, I'm sure. Here is a guy with a wife and two kids. He's got a job that will keep him in demand in the years to come—people will always need shoes, and the stocks in the shoestores won't last forever. Why should he uproot his entire family to take a chance on a wild venture like ours? Can't say I blame him —it's a hard decision to make, sometimes. You and I, without ties, are lucky. We can pick up and go when and where we please. Be careful what responsibilities you take on."

"What do we do now, then?" Peter asked.

"We move on. We've still got a lot of ground to cover, and I don't have any more pressing business in L.A. As soon as Kudjo shows up with a scouting report and we can get everybody back into the cars, we'll leave."

Kudjo arrived back half an hour later. He said the freeway was clear all the way through to the east side of the city and there didn't appear to be any gangs to make trouble. With that assurance, everyone got into their respective cars. Honon, who had a walkie-talkie link-up to each vehicle, gave the word and the caravan started off again. Peter, at Honon's invitation, rode in the cab of the lead truck with the caravan leader.

The cars proceeded along the road at a casual forty miles per hour, staying in the righthand lane. Very occasionally another car would pass them, but they encountered little traffic compared to what the freeway had once carried. Interstate 5 skirted the

48

northern edge of the city, passing through once-lush hills now swarming with shanty towns, and industrial areas that were all but deserted. As they drove, Honon related some personal anecdotes; there were so many, and they were so colorful, that Peter decided to believe only half of them.

They had gone twenty-five miles, just past the junction with the Pasadena Freeway, when Honon glanced in his sideview mirror and gave a low whistle. "Uh oh, trouble."

"What's the matter?" Peter started to say; then he saw the flashing red lights on the motorcycle that drew up alongside them, and he knew.

During the early days of the Collapse, the crime rate had soared beyond all imaginable limits. A frightened public had demanded action, which eventually came in the form of strengthened police departments and tough laws. They thought repression would provide the order they needed in their lives—and for a while it did. But it was like putting on a Band-Aid to hide the first leprous patch of skin.

The breakdown in government meant an inability to pay police salaries, but did not necessarily end the "law enforcement" institution. The police uniform was universally respected and feared, and the men wearing it quickly learned that their uniform and gun could get them anything they wanted. Public protectors became public predators; policemen nowadays were little more than thugs with uniforms.

Complying with the request of the officer on the motorcycle, Honon pulled his truck over to the side of the freeway. The other cars in the caravan pulled over as well; staying together was the most important thing. Honon took a battered leather wallet out of his pocket. "Hopefully all he'll want is some cash and we can be on our way again," he told Peter. "If he wants more than that, we're in for trouble."

The cop sidled over to Honon's door. He stood only about five foot five, but looked tough and wiry. He kept his goggles on and wore his black leather jacket like a commission direct from God. His holster was unsnapped, the gun ready to be drawn and fired at an instant's notice. "What's goin' on here?" he asked.

"Some friends of mine and I were just passing through town," Honon said jovially. "Nothing against that, is there?"

"That remains to be seen. Where you from?"

"San Francisco."

"Where you headed?"

"San Diego."

"Why?"

"Why not? It seemed as good a place as any."

The officer contemplated that. "Maybe. I've heard things aren't so good down there, though."

"Things aren't good anywhere, so we thought we might as well take our pick of bad places."

"I don't like stoners," the cop said. "Trouble-makers, every one of them. I try to run a peaceful sector, and I can't do it with all the stoners traipsin' through, stirrin' things up. I particularly don't like groups of stoners. If one's bad, a gang's worse. You were goin' too slow."

"I beg your pardon."

"Can't you see that sign? The speed limit's fifty-five on the freeways. I clocked you going forty."

"We were in the righthand lane and there wasn't any traffic. We didn't think it would matter."

"Matters to me," the cop said. "Let's see, we've got seven vehicles here, that's seven movin' violations. You got a parade license?"

"I didn't think we needed one."

"Anything more than five vehicles constitutes a parade. That's the law." Peter doubted that, but left all dealings with the patrolman up to Honon—he obviously had encountered problems like this before.

"Do all these people have driver's licenses?" the cop asked next.

"Of course they do," Honon responded without hesitation.

The policeman paused for a moment. Apparently he was debating whether it was worth his time and energy to go back along the row and check with every single driver whether that was so. He finally decided to skip that—he had enough charges already. He pulled an official-looking pad out of his hip pocket and wrote in it. "Let's see, that's seven counts of obstructin' traffic and one of leadin' a parade without a license. Fine'll be three hundred and fifty dollars."

Peter drew in a quick breath when he heard that, but Honon didn't even blink. The big man calmly reached into his wallet and pulled out six fifty dollar bills, two twenties and a ten. "This should cover it," he said.

The officer stared at the proffered money. "Where'd you get all that?" he asked. "Rob a bank or somethin'?"

"We pooled our life savings to make this trip."

51

The officer looked back in the direction of the camper. "You got any food back there?"

"Not much, no. Just enough for ourselves for the next day or so."

The cop's hand moved up to his hip, resting on the butt of his pistol. The fingers twitched nervously. "Come on out of there *slowly* and lead me back there. I want to see this for myself."

As Honon stepped out of the cab the policeman moved back slightly. He apparently hadn't realized the man he was talking to was as big and powerful as that, and wanted to take no chances. He pulled his gun and held it loose at his side. "You go ahead of me and don't try any tricks. I'll have you covered all the way."

Honon walked along the row of cars with the cop two steps behind him. Just as he passed the cab of the second armored truck, Kudjo swung its door quickly open, coming between Honon and the policeman. Honon ducked for cover under the truck at the same moment the startled cop raised his gun and fired. His shot ricocheted off the bulletproof door and hit him in the stomach. The gun dropped from his hand as he crumpled limply to the ground.

"Hey, man," Kudjo shouted to Honon, "you can come out from under there. This gent ain't gonna hurt nobody right now."

Honon crawled back out as the other caravan members, including Peter, rushed over to see what the outcome had been. "I thought you were going to jump him and beat him up," said John Gianelli, age ten.

"That would have taken too much energy,"

Honon explained. "It's always better to let your opponent fight himself. Most of them will. Remember that." He bent down and removed the policeman's holster, put the gun back into it and handed the ensemble to Peter. "Here, a present for you— a .38 police special. Know how to use it?"

"Not really," Peter admitted.

"You'll probably learn before the trip's over. I think I've got some ammo for that in the back of the first truck."

Peter took the proffered items uncertainly. "What do we do now?"

"We confiscate his motorcycle, then get the hell out of here. There's always the chance a few of his buddies may be around, and I don't want to be here when they arrive to check out the sound of that shot."

"But this man's hurt," Risa Svenson protested from the back of the crowd. "He could die here."

Honon snorted. "Then his fellow jackals can pick his bones. He's not my concern—you are. I want everybody back in their cars and ready to roll as soon as Kudjo and I get this motorcycle into the first truck. That's an order!"

CHAPTER 4

It is conceivable that within three decades, a time-span most of us will witness, the operation of, say, an electric can opener without an expensive permit will be seen as a crime against society, punished as severely as is grand theft today. No matter what new veins or pools of fossil fuels may be discovered, the cost of keeping comfortable with central heating, air conditioning and electric appliances will continue to explode if alternate energy sources are not exploited.

—Moneysworth
16 September 1974

Transportation is the second of the Big Three. Our civilization is utterly dependent on the movement of people from one place to another. Lack of fuel leads to lack of movement, and without this movement one of the main pillars of society will crumble. . . .

Think of all the people directly or indirectly connected with transportation. At first glance, their numbers look small—bus drivers, cab drivers, airplane pilots and stewardesses. But then take a look at the vacation industry—there are whole towns that would lose their income if transportation were halted because their economy is geared to tourism. When the tourists vanish, a lot of people will be left with nothing to do. . . .

The disappearance of tourism, though, is only the tip of the iceberg. In recent years, retail outlets have concentrated themselves in large shopping centers, on the theory that people would rather make one long trip to do all their shopping than a number of smaller ones. What happens to these places—and their employees—when nobody can make any trips except on foot or by bicycle? Business falls off when there's a gasoline shortage, putting people out of jobs and generally depressing the economy. . . .

What happens to the factory when its workers have no gas to drive their cars to work and public transportation is on strike? The answer is simple —it stops producing whatever it had been manufacturing, no matter how badly its products are needed. . . .

—Peter Stone
World Collapse

*　　*　　*

"Are we really going to San Diego?" Peter asked as Honon started up the armored truck.

The big man shot him a suspicious look. "Of course not; we're not even getting close. But I didn't want that clown to be able to track us too easily in case he survives and tells his friends about us. Misdirection is always easier than fighting."

55

About one mile further on, the caravan transferred from Interstate 5 to Interstate 10, also known as the San Bernardino Freeway. The direction also changed, from southeast to almost due east. The route went through many small suburb communities, some of the seventy-odd independent towns that made up Los Angeles County.

After traveling through a mountain pass and some more suburbs, Honon pulled the armored truck over to the side of the road. The other vehicles in the procession followed his example, and soon they were all lined up off the roadway. It was now late afternoon and the sinking sun was casting long shadows in front of them. "Is something the matter?" Peter asked. "Why are we stopping?"

In answer, Honon pointed at the gas gauge, which registered just over a quarter of a tank. "We're getting low," he said, "and since we're about to pass into wilderness territory I'd like to refill here. And *that* is a major undertaking. Besides, we should have something to eat before continuing on." Since they hadn't eaten since breakfast, Peter's stomach made no objection.

Charlie Itsobu fixed up another meal for the travelers. It was hearty and filling, but heavy on vegetables and low on protein. The fact that the caravan was on a two-meal-a-day schedule was upsetting to the children, although Honon assured people that the situation was slightly more normal back in the Monastery. To Peter, who had recently had to scramble to get a single meal a day, this situation was a vast improvement.

Kudjo Wilson ate a very quick dinner, conferring with Honon all the while. When he was finished, he took off down the freeway on his motorcycle. "Where's he going now?" Peter asked, to which Honon cheerfully replied, "Looking for a gas station."

After dinner the caravan members gathered around the camper truck, questioning Honon about the Monastery. They never seemed to tire of hearing about this Paradise and Honon, though he must have told the story hundreds of times before to different groups of people, still managed to put life into his narrative. At the same time, he retained the aura of secrecy about the Monastery's location, but the people were used to that.

The sun had set and dusk had almost become dark when Kudjo returned. He conferred some more with Honon, who then began rounding up the men of the expedition. "Come on, Peter," he said, "vacation's over. You've got some work to do."

"What are we up to?"

"We're going to get us some gasoline."

Kudjo, Charlie Itsobu, Dom Gianelli, Bill Lavochek and Harvey Parks all piled into the back of the lead armored truck, while Honon motioned for Peter to get in front. He had, apparently, taken Peter on as a favorite, feeling the need to explain things to him. Peter supposed it was because he was an independent critic and Honon wanted to justify this nomadic existence to him.

Before leaving Honon had a short talk with Sarah Finkelstein, whom he put in charge of the caravan while he was gone. Sarah nodded and Honon, satisfied, came back to the armored truck, jumped in the driver's seat and started the engine.

"Are we going to steal the gas?" Peter asked.

"Not if you can think of any other way to get it."

"I don't suppose they'd take money."

"Not in my experience, which has been quite extensive. We've got plenty of cash—we did rob a bank, by the way, but the citizens of that community were so far into bartering they didn't care what happened to those little green slips of paper. But not many people are taking cash these days. Besides, these smaller communities may only have a gas tanker go through here every other month or so; they have to hoard every drop. Even if they were taking cash, they couldn't afford to fill us seven vehicles at any price."

"So, in effect, you're killing these communities to keep yourself going."

Honon gave him a quizzical glance. "Are you moralizing at me after all the things you wrote in your book?"

"Not exactly. I just like to keep everything in perspective, that's all. It's too easy a temptation to say that the end justifies the means. Every time I hear that, I take a close look at the situation to see whether it really does."

The big man nodded. "I never said this was justified. But it *is* necessary if we're to get where we're going. If the trip isn't worth the fare, I can put you on your bicycle and we'll call it even."

"It isn't that," Peter said, shaking his head. "I know it's a cruel world out there. I predicted it, remember? But if we're supposed to be 'keeping Civilization alive,' it might be best to keep the rules in mind."

"The rules of Civilization apply only when there are other civilized people around you. The world we're in now isn't civilized, and if you try to play with outmoded rules you'll end up getting your teeth kicked in."

Honon paused to let that sink in, then continued, "I like to think of myself as an agent of Evolution. The supply of gasoline is virtually nil now; it will have dried up completely in three months. These people are going to have to get along without it sooner or later. I'm just hastening the day when they'll have to learn to be self-sufficient. Maybe I'm even giving them a jump on their neighbors, who knows? But the fittest will survive; they always do."

"You're a fine one to talk about self-sufficiency— you're more dependent on gasoline than any of these people are."

"I thought you'd catch me up on that one. Yes, I have given it some thought. This is the last recruiting drive I'll be doing by car; if there's time for any more before the starship takes off I'll go around with horses and covered wagons, just like in the frontier days. I could keep off the roads that way and avoid a lot of trouble. But I couldn't resist one last try at a mechanized caravan." He pulled the truck up an offramp and onto a surface street. A waxing gibbous moon illuminated the area, and he turned out his headlights to avoid being seen. There was virtually no other traffic here, and the biggest danger was of being spotted by a suspicious local citizen.

Finally he pulled over to the side of the street and shut off the motor. "End of the line," he announced. "We go on foot from here."

They let the other men out of the back and Peter got his first look inside. In addition to the scouting motorcycles the armored truck was carrying an arsenal—rifles, pistols, machine guns, grenades and a few other shapes that he couldn't identify in the darkness. Honon didn't give him much time to gawk. "Have you got your .38?" Peter nodded. "Safety off?" Honon continued.

"Uh, I don't know."

Honon checked it quickly. "Yeah, it's off. You shouldn't have been carrying it that way. Remind me when I've got a spare second and I'll teach you something about it.

"The indoctrination lesson for this raid is short and simple—if you use your gun, mean it. And if you do use it, you'd damn well better have a good reason, or I'll take it out of your ass when we get back. Understand?"

He didn't wait for the answer. Instead, he grabbed his walkie-talkie and held it up to his face. "Okay, Sarah, we're going in on foot now. Get the rest of the caravan driven up as far as the offramp and wait." He listened for her acknowledgement, then clicked the set off and clipped it to his belt. Grabbing a machine gun and slinging its strap over his shoulder, he told his group, "Come on."

They proceeded slowly and quietly down the street, keeping to the shadows as much as possible. This seemed to be primarily a residential neighborhood, given over to single family houses that were following what seemed to be the universal pattern—lawns converted into small gardens as people strove desperately to maintain their independence from the outside world. There was no one visible as they moved along; no one in their right minds would be out wandering after sundown, nor would they have reason to. There was no place to go any more.

Occasionally a dog would bark as they passed a house, causing them to start, but it was always a false alarm. Dogs were invariably kept inside the houses; they were needed as protection for the owners, and they were too valuable to let out at night when there was a risk of dognapping. If the raiding party was observed on its way down the street, no alarm was raised.

The gas station was a quarter mile from where they'd left their vehicle. It sat on a corner of the street, dark and brooding, as though it knew its days were numbered. Barbed wire fences eight feet high completely surrounded it except for the driveways, which were currently locked with chain link gates. The station was dark because the community did not have the power to keep it lit—but dark certainly did not mean unguarded.

While Honon held the rest of the group back, Kudjo took a pair of wire cutters and moved stealthily toward the station. So adept was he with his work that even Peter, who knew he was there and where he was going, lost him from sight after a few moments. He was just another part of the shadows now, albeit a deadly part.

The men waited silently for fifteen minutes. They could not see Kudjo working, but Peter guessed that the young black was doing his usual effective job. Then all of a sudden Kudjo materialized at his elbow, scaring the wits out of him. "Easy, man," Kudjo grinned. "We don't want you jumpin' at spooks." To Honon he said, "We're all set to move."

The leader nodded. "Remember," he told his men, "I'd *strongly* prefer no shooting. Let's go in there and do our job."

As a unit the men moved forward, following Kudjo's lead. He took them around to the side of the station, where he'd cut a hole two feet wide and three feet high in the barbed wire. "There's two men in the office," he whispered, "and at least two more in the service bay, possibly as many as five."

Honon nodded. "Kudjo, I want you, Dom, Harvey, Charlie and Bill to take the service bay. Peter and I'll hit the office. As soon as we're through the fence, on the count of three."

The men squeezed through the hole single file, and when all of them were on the other side Honon began his count. On three they all jumped forward, running quickly through the darkness on their toes to minimize the noise. Peter thought the beating of his heart alone would alert the guards, it was so strong.

Reaching the door to the office, Honon gave the knob a quick turn and a push. The door flew open inwards and the big man rushed inside. Peter was barely a step behind.

As Kudjo had told them there were two men there, shadowy figures in the darkness behind a desk. The attack had taken them completely by surprise, they didn't even have time to react before the two from the caravan were upon them. By unspoken agreement, Honon went after the man on the left; one quick uppercut from the big man's fist left that guard unconscious. Peter, not as sure of his own abilities, hit his man across the face with his gun butt. The end result was the same—two kayoes in as many seconds.

A smashing of glass sounded outside. Honon had not even stopped, but had reached for the door that led from the office to the service bay. Peter realized that the other men had the harder task—the only ways to get into the repair area were through the garage doors and through the office. With the former down, the invaders would have to break through the glass—giving the guards warning enough to take action.

There were no lights in the service bay, either— just dim shadows shifting in the moonlight. Dark shapes leaped through the area of broken glass into the bay, but once they were inside the darkness gobbled them up. Now Peter could see why Honon was so opposed to the use of their weapons. Not only did he want to make as little noise as possible, but he didn't want any of his own people shot by mistake. In these shadows, it was impossible to tell friend from foe at more than a foot away.

"Move carefully to your right," Honon whispered to Peter. "If anything moves, or if you see someone you don't recognize, hit him first and worry about it later." Peter saw the wisdom of the plan. If all the men from the caravan moved in a counterclockwise direction and made one or two full circuits, they should have flushed out all the guards that were hiding in the area.

Across the bay he heard the smacking sound of flesh against flesh, followed by a short groan. There was no way of knowing, though, which side had been the victor in that struggle. He kept moving slowly, checking every shadow for suspicious signs.

A shape that had first appeared part of a work table suddenly leaped out at him. The attack caught him off balance; he stepped back to get out of the way and nearly slipped on a spot of grease. The guard grabbed him and knocked him to the ground. He would probably have knocked Peter out in another moment had not Honon arrived just then. With one blow, the defender was out cold. Honon reached a hand down to help Peter up. Peter started to thank him, but the big man just said, "Keep on moving."

The eerie battle went on in silence for thirty minutes, during which time Peter made three complete circuits of the area. Occasionally he would hear the sound of a scuffle somewhere, but he had no idea of who was winning this unusual fight. He himself took part in no further action, but by the end of the half hour his eyestrain was so acute that every dark shape took on sinister proportions and every shadow seemed alive.

Finally Honon said aloud, "I think that should do it." A flashlight beam snapped on, and Peter had to wince at its intensity after so long a period of staring into the darkness. The beam played around the floor, revealing the bodies of four strangers lying unconscious on the ground.

"If you had a flashlight," Peter said, "why didn't you use it before and spare us this ring-around-the-rosie?"

"Because I didn't want them shooting at us. As long as both sides were in the dark, they probably thought they had an equal chance, and they wouldn't want to give their own positions away by firing. If they thought for a second that we had an advantage, they'd have had nothing to lose by shooting—which might have brought other people from the neighborhood." He turned away from Peter and unclipped the walkie-talkie from his belt. "Okay, Sarah, we're in. Bring them on up—slowly and quietly."

While Honon had been talking, Kudjo was busy searching the bodies of the unconscious guards. His search met with success and he held up a ring of keys. Honon nodded at him. "You unlock the gate and I'll go back and get our truck. With any luck, we'll be gone in half an hour."

There was nothing much for Peter to do now but stand around and make sure none of the guards regained consciousness. If any of them stirred, he had orders to tie him up and gag him; but none of the men twitched and he had no chance to do even that much. After only a couple of minutes the rest of the cars in the caravan—driven by Jason Tagon and the women—drove up. Kudjo swung the gates open for them and they lined up in an orderly procession to be refueled.

It took just twenty minutes to replenish all seven

gas tanks, but they hung around for a few minutes longer because several of the members wanted to take advantage of this situation to use a civilized rest room. Finally, though, they were ready to roll and Honon gave the order to move out. He himself stayed behind with Peter so that when the last vehicle had left he could lock the gates up behind it and toss the keys back into the service station area. "I don't want to be any worse on those people than I have to be," he explained. "Leaving the gates open would only invite other robbers less moral than we are."

"Do you think they'll chase us?"

"Perhaps, but not very far if they do. Remember, their fuel supply has just been seriously depleted. They'll probably want to cut their losses and keep this from happening again."

"Won't that make it harder for you the next time you come through here?"

"Nope. I make it a point never to go the same route twice. It avoids gaining a reputation."

The caravan returned to Interstate 10 and continued eastward for several hours. They were leaving the urban area of Los Angeles behind and entering desert country. They met with no other traffic as they made their peaceful way along the road.

Finally, just outside Palm Springs, Honon called a halt. "That's enough for one night. We'll stop here, get a bit of rest and wait until breakfast. Then there's a man I want to see, an engineer who might make a good recruit."

Peter leaned back in his seat and was asleep before he knew it. The excitement and exercise of the previous day were more than he was accustomed to, and had worn him out quite thoroughly. The next thing he knew, Marcia Konigsburg was shaking his shoulder and offering him breakfast. He sat up groggily, thanked her and went outside to eat with the others.

Honon had already left on his recruitment mission and Kudjo was off scouting the road ahead. There was nothing else to do but get better acquainted with the people he was sharing the ride with. In particular, Peter was haunted by thoughts of Risa Svenson, the odd blonde girl who had affected him so strongly the day before.

During the morning the children ran and played alongside the caravan, but as the day wore on and the sun beat down with increasingly more heat, most activity more strenuous than talking was halted. Kudjo returned at two-thirty in the afternoon to find virtually everyone in the camp on siesta, and proceeded to take a nap himself.

Honon's cycle wasn't spotted returning until close to sunset. Right behind him was a late model Cadillac, being driven by a man nobody recognized. "I knew he'd be back in time for dinner," Kudjo commented.

Honon and his follower made a U-turn, crossing the divider section and coming to a stop behind the caravan. Naturally, everyone gathered around their leader to greet the new arrival. "I'd like you all to meet Gregor Ilyich Zhepanin," Honon said by way of introduction. "Gregor is a nuclear propulsion engineer and he'll be coming with us."

That name rang a bell in Peter's mind, but it took a second before he was able to place it. Zhepanin had been a noted space expert in his native Russia until his outspoken political views made him anathema to the Communist Party. He disappeared from the scene for a while, and there was even some speculation that the KGB had had him secretly killed and disposed of. Then all of a sudden, ten years ago, he turned up in the United States amid international scandals and rumors of CIA involvement, claiming that he had defected and requesting political asylum. He had been a focal point for news writers for two years after that, with a widely publicized marriage that ended almost as quickly as it began and a reputation for giving fiery, anticommunist speeches that were almost as embarrassing to the U.S. government as they were to the Russians. Then Zhepanin had faded from the popular press while other, more crucial stories edged their way in.

Peter took a careful look at this newcomer. Zhepanin was a man in his early forties, of medium height and build. His clean-shaven face, which tended to jowliness, was topped by an unkempt thatch of dark hair. He had dark, piggy eyes that appeared ready to brood at a moment's notice. At present, those eyes were darting nervously back and forth as they took in this unfamiliar scene.

People in the crowd, sensing Zhepanin's nervousness, tried their best to be jovial and outgoing, but that only upset the Russian more. "Please forgive me, I am no longer accustomed to meeting so many people at once," he said. "I would like some time to be alone, after which I am sure we will all become good friends."

He started to make his way through the crowd,

which parted obligingly for him, when he spotted Peter. He stopped and looked, recognition evident on his face. "You are Peter Stone, are you not? The fellow who wrote that book about the end of Civilization?" Peter nodded.

With a scowl of contempt, Zhepanin turned his head and walked coldly away from Peter. The rest of the group was taken aback at this odd treatment, and even Peter was not sure how to react. Finally Honon ended the silence as his booming voice proclaimed: "I don't know about everyone else, but I'm starving. Let's have some dinner so we can get this show on the road!"

CHAPTER 5

The tendency to increasing disorder (entropy) is universal. . . . It is reasonable to assume that the more people I depend on, the less secure is my existence. There are too many factors that must simultaneously be right; more potential points of failure. If one person goes berserk, an increasing number suffer. We are becoming more susceptible to human carelessness—and human madness.

—J. Calvin Giddings
Bulletin of the Atomic Scientists
September, 1973

We all fear the system. We all see how large and impersonal it's become. There are simply too many people in society for government to be able to respond to all their needs; it must, of necessity, grow callous. This leads people to say, "The system is out to get me, so I'll get it first." It becomes acceptable to cheat on one's income tax or lie to get welfare. It becomes not only reasonable but mandatory for workers to strike to better their living conditions, no matter what hardships those strikes bring to other, perfectly innocent, members of society.

We are becoming a world of "me-firsters," where the good of the individual frequently conflicts with the good of the society. And within the framework of a civilization that absolutely requires perfect cooperation between its various elements, this can have only one, disastrous, conclusion. . . .

—Peter Stone
World Collapse

*   *   *

No further mention was made of Zhepanin's behavior, though it had obviously affected the atmosphere in the camp. Dinner was eaten quickly and quietly, with none of the usual long conversations or speculations on the future.

Honon usually allowed about an hour after the meal was finished before scheduling "move out." This allowed time for the food to settle and for people to relieve themselves before the traveling started once again. Peter went over to Risa and asked her if she would like to take a short stroll with him. He was half expecting her to decline the offer, and was quite surprised when she accepted.

The two walked across the sand a short distance away from the highway, making sure to keep the caravan in sight at all times. At first nothing was said, but finally Peter felt compelled to break the silence. "I told you the story of my life yesterday," he began awkwardly, "yet I hardly know anything about you."

"There's not much to tell. I'm nineteen years old, and the only living relative I have is my mother in

Tucson. I left home when I was seventeen, without even finishing high school, to go out to California. I guess I thought it was supposed to be more exciting there or something. I wrote to my mother several times, but the mail was getting really bad then and I never got an answer. Honon won't tell me whether we're going through Tucson or not, so I don't know when I'll get to see her again.

"About the only thing I do really well is make pottery. I had a small stand off the road just outside Monterey; that's where Kudjo found me and asked me if I'd like to come along on this trip. I said yes, and here I am."

Peter looked at her. She was so slender and frail, and so childlike in her innocence, that he felt an overwhelming desire to wrap her in cotton candy and protect her from reality. He put a nervous hand around her waist; she accepted it without question and leaned her body against him. "Why did you agree to come along?" he asked her.

She didn't answer immediately, but gazed out into the desert in a thoughtful mood. Finally she said, "I guess it's because I'm an optimist, basically. I want to believe in happy endings, and there wasn't going to be one in Monterey."

"Do you think there'll be one on this new world they have planned out for us?"

Risa shrugged. "I don't know. But it sounds so exciting, doesn't it? A whole new world that no one has ever seen before. New animals, new foods, new plants. A new chance to be people, I don't like being forced to be a number. On the new world, we'll all have to act like human beings again."

Peter gave a sarcastic grunt. "Some help that'll be!"

She turned and looked up into his face, locking his gaze with her own. "Then why are you coming, if you don't think a new beginning is going to help us?"

Her eyes were so warm and blue that they muddled his thinking and softened his sarcasm. "There doesn't seem to be much left here for us, so that would be as good a place as any to be. I can't share your blind faith in the goodness of Humanity, Risa; I've seen too much of it. There are some good people and there are some good goals to work towards. I do the best I can, without demanding that others come up to my hopes or expectations. I try not to be too disappointed when things go badly, because I know there are times when they're bound to. I want to hope, but I know that hoping too much can hurt."

Risa sighed, but did not take her gaze away from his. "Please try not to be too sarcastic, Peter." Her voice was almost pleading. "You're so much nicer as a person than as a cynic."

As he looked down into her eyes, he suddenly found his arms surrounding her and his head bending down to hers. Their lips met in a tentative kiss that evolved gradually as more and more passion flowed through them. They stood there in the desert, locked in each other's embrace, until someone from the caravan sounded a horn, calling them back.

Zhepanin's Cadillac was added to the end of the line as the caravan moved out. Because of the long, hard day Honon had put in, he let Peter drive the first truck that night. It had been a long time since Peter had driven anything more complex than a bicycle, and the truck's controls took a bit of refamiliarization. But once he did get going he did a competent job of traveling the route Honon laid out for him.

A short way past Palm Springs, at Indio, the caravan turned off Interstate 10 and began moving southward again on California 86. The road, of course, was not lit and Peter couldn't see anything beyond the range of his headlights so he had no idea what sort of country they were passing through. Whatever it was, though, it was pretty barren; absolutely no traffic passed them and the only noises were the sounds of their own cars.

After several hours they came to a sign telling them that they were passing through the town of Brawley, but the community made no impression on them and they didn't even slow down. A little further along the road they came to the town of El Centro where, in accordance with Honon's instructions, Peter turned the caravan eastward again onto Interstate 8. They were now heading out into real desert country and, Peter suspected, a drive along the southern portion of Arizona. He still had no idea where the Monastery was located, but he knew that if he himself had wanted to hide a secret colony of several thousand people, the deserts of the great American Southwest would be an ideal spot—except for a lack of a water supply.

As Honon had instructed, Peter brought the caravan to a halt right after crossing the Colorado River into Arizona. They passed a border guard station that appeared deserted, and Honon breathed a sigh of relief. "A lot of border guards are turning into pirates," he said, "and if you want to cross over their line you have to pay their price. Not much we can do about it, except hope they're not there."

They were now just outside Yuma, where Honon said he had another candidate to recruit. He suggested that they get some sleep in preparation for the next day and Peter, exhausted from several hours of boring night driving, fully agreed.

With the first light of morning they awoke and went outside for breakfast. Zhepanin was out there in the chow line, apparently used to the new company now. He was trying to overcome the bad initial impression he had made the day before by being cheerful and talkative; on the whole, he appeared successful, with people introducing themselves in the same friendly manner as during Peter's first breakfast. In particular he was making a hit with the children, telling them old Russian folk-tales that they'd never heard before. When he caught sight of Peter, however, he scowled and turned to face the other direction.

"Is there something between you two I don't know about?" Honon asked, concerned about this ill-feeling in the ranks of his caravan.

"Beats me," Peter said. "I never met the man before in my life."

"Hmmm. Well, I'll have a talk with him and find out what the matter is. Don't let it worry you."

"I won't. Too many people already hate me; one more won't make any difference."

They stood in line and eventually got their breakfast. Peter passed up a couple of invitations to sit and eat with various people, going instead off to the side of the road by himself. As he ate, he watched Honon approach Zhepanin and take him aside for a talk. They were just barely within earshot, and by straining his hearing Peter could make out what they were saying.

"You did not tell me that Peter Stone was with your group," Zhepanin complained.

"I didn't tell you I weigh two hundred and fifteen pounds, either. I didn't know it mattered to you."

"It does." Zhepanin cast a dirty look in the direction of Peter, who pretended to be concentrating on his food. "He is an animal, a man striving for despotism and collectivism. That is what I left Russia for, to get away from such men. I thought that here, in America, I would be free to do as I like. What do I find? That man advocating the end of free enterprise, a socialist state that kills old people and tells the survivors what they can eat, where they can live, how many children they can have—even Russia was not as bad as that."

"He's entitled to his opinion, isn't he?"

"He is a Communist, and I have had my fill of Communists." The conversation went on further, but at this point Marcia Konigsburg came over and began nattering to Peter about some trivial thing or other so that he could no longer hear what the two men were saying. By the time Marcia flitted away again, the two men had moved out of his hearing range.

Wandering back into the camp, Peter learned that

Jason Tagon had declared today to be Sunday. For all Peter knew, he could be right. Time had little meaning in a nonagricultural, nonbusiness society, and Peter had lost track of the days of the week and the exact month quite some time ago. Much to his surprise, he'd found that he didn't miss them, either. What did it matter whether today was really Tuesday, Friday or Sunday if you had nothing scheduled for any of them?

But to the religious among the group it did matter. Jason celebrated a Mass with the Gianellis and the Lavocheks, and Peter noted to his mild chagrin that Risa sat in on the service though she didn't take part in the makeshift communion. It was more of that blind faith of hers, he supposed, in which he could never share.

After hearing confession for a couple of minutes —after all, how many sins could people commit in this limited social milieu?—Jason come over to Peter. "I have a personal problem that needs talking out," he said, "and since I don't have a confessor of my own along I need someone I can discuss it with. Would you mind lending an ear?"

"Not at all. I've been accused of loving to give too much advice; people never seem to take it, but I'm still open to consultation."

The two men walked a short distance from the line of cars. "It's about my vow of chastity," Jason said. "When I took it I meant every word I said, but the situation has changed somewhat. If I am to go along to Epsilon Eridani with the rest of the colonists, I know I won't be allowed to keep it. The practicalities of the situation will require maximum use of the gene pool, and I will have to procreate along with everyone else to help build the world."

Peter nodded. "I see. And dispensations will be hard to come by on another planet."

"Precisely. You can't even get in touch with the Pope from *here*." He scowled as a thought suddenly occured to him. "I wonder if there even is a Pope, any more. The entire Vatican could have sunk into the earth and I would never know about it."

"Does it matter?"

"I suppose not," Jason shrugged. "I'm still one of God's children. My love of Him and my free will are both intact. It's just that one gets used to a certain hierarchical structure."

"If I were your God," Peter said slowly, "I would realize that situations change, sometimes drastically. I would not hold a man to his oath if the circumstances surrounding that oath have turned about."

"You're oversimplifying a terribly complex situation. . . ."

"Perhaps, but making something too complicated prevents you from seeing answers, too. Look at it another way. The Church condemns suicide by individuals, which would seem to indicate that racial suicide is also wrong. Unnatural celibacy in a survival situation would lead, in the long run, to racial suicide, the most mortal sin of all."

"Your arguments sound slick, but I'm not sure they're correct."

"That's because they're corollaries to the main argument—namely, that we are not operating in the world we grew up with. Our behavior is dictated by a system of values that is now dead. Well, maybe 'dormant' would be a better word; the whole point of this caravan, the Monastery, the starship is to make sure that those values ultimately survive. But until then we're playing a new game with different rules. If we ignore these changes, we won't live long enough to restore the old ways."

"I know what it is to have a nagging conscience. I felt awfully queasy about robbing that gas station, but I would—and probably will—do it again if I must in order to get to the Monastery."

Jason nodded slowly, but made no comment. The silence dragged on for over a minute before he finally spoke. "I can't say I agree with you completely. I was brought up as an absolutist, that some things are always right and others always wrong, no matter what the circumstances. That kind of training is hard to break. I recognize the need to rob gas stations, though I will not participate myself. I will not attack and steal from another man whose need may be as great as my own."

"That doesn't absolve you."

"I know," Jason said in a barely audible voice. His hands were trembling as he turned to walk back to the caravan. "I want to thank you for having this talk with me. It's straightened out a couple of questions in my own mind—and, of course, raised a host of new ones."

"That seems to be my purpose in life," said Peter. "Giving people advice they don't like. At least you had the decency to thank me for it."

Honon had left on his recruiting mission by the time Peter got back to the caravan, so there was no opportunity to find out precisely where matters stood with Zhepanin. The Russian was not in sight, probably sleeping in one of the cars. That idea sounded so tempting that Peter decided to get some sleep himself. Curling up in the passenger seat of the lead truck, he dropped quickly into unconsciousness.

Honon returned slightly after noon with a young man riding behind him on the motorcycle. Peter had awakened from his nap just a few minutes before, and went out to greet them, along with several of the other members who were awake.

The newcomer was tall and thin—"gangly" was the word that came to Peter's mind—with a thick mane of blond hair and the greenest, most intense eyes Peter had ever seen. He had a ruggedly handsome face and a self-confident bearing. Peter guessed him to be in his late twenties.

"This is Lee Mercer," Honon introduced. "He's quite a talented architect, according to the people who recommended him. He studied at Mrs. Frank Lloyd Wright's academy, Taliesin West, for awhile, before it fell apart like everything else. I think that's a pretty impressive credential. Lee, these people will all inundate you with their names at their own convenience, so I won't bother with a lot of introductions that you won't remember anyhow."

"I recognize Mr. Stone over there. I never missed a chance to watch him debate on television."

Peter made a slight, sarcastic bow. "I knew I had a fan somewhere."

"I was just in favor of anyone who had the guts to rattle the Establishment."

As Peter watched and listened to this new fellow,

alarm bells went off in his mind. There was nothing specific he could point to—just a delicate, fluid quality to his speech, and the attitude at which he carried his body—but Peter became convinced that Lee Mercer was gay. Did Honon know that? He glanced at the caravan leader, but there was nothing in the big man's manner to reveal anything one way or the other.

The newcomer's sexual preferences did not bother Peter much; what did concern him was how the other caravan members would react when they discovered the truth. Some of them seemed uptight enough to cause trouble, and he wanted to make sure Honon was prepared for it.

The big man took him aside shortly after leaving Lee to get acquainted on his own. "I think you'd better stay out of Zhepanin's way for awhile," he said.

"Because he thinks I'm a Communist?"

"So you heard that, eh? No, it's more than just that. Like most people, he tends to look on you as a scapegoat, as the bringer of destruction to a world in which he'd carved out a comfortable niche for himself. Here he was, a man who had reached the top of his profession at a young age—almost as young as when you reached yours—and who had managed to escape from the society that held him back. In the U.S. he was able to accumulate wealth and prestige—until the Collapse came. He blames you."

"Why should he be any different?"

"I'm not asking you to like the man, any more than I'm asking him to like you. I'd just like you to stay out of his way until we get to the Monastery, for the interests of the group. We need him, Peter; he's *the* top man in the field of nuclear propulsion. And we can't afford to quarrel among ourselves in the middle of hostile territory."

"I'll go along with that, and I'll try to stay out of his path. But while we're on the subject of internal quarreling, you may have brought a beauty of a fight with you into the camp. Are you aware that Lee is gay?"

Honon didn't even blink. "Yes, he told me so at the outset of our conversation. He makes no particular secret of it. He was a militant before the troubles hit, and still espouses 'gay pride.' " His eyes narrowed. "Does it make a difference to you?"

"Not personally, but how will the rest of the people react?"

"Well, it'll give them something to talk about at dinner, won't it?" Honon flashed him a weary smile. "I've been traveling with these people for a lot longer than you have. They've got their prejudices and hangups, sure; who doesn't? But on the whole they are people of reason. I think there'll be an initial dust-up and then they'll forget it. Right now, though, I refuse to worry about it. I want to get some sleep. We've got to get more gas tonight, and I want to be awake for that."

He turned and walked off toward the lead truck. Watching him go, Peter suddenly understood the fatigue and loneliness of the man. The shoulders drooped and the gait was a weary shuffle when, as now, he thought nobody was watching. He alone was responsible for the care and safety of more than twenty people through hazardous, sometimes even hostile, conditions. When danger presented itself or a figure of authority was needed, Honon could throw off his fatigue like an old blanket. But even a bear needed rest sometime, and Honon was getting precious little of it. *I hope he doesn't kill himself before this expedition's over,* Peter thought sympathetically.

The test of Honon's theories came at dinnertime. Peter and Honon were eating their evening meal with Jason, Risa and the Gianellis when Harvey Parks approached them. "Uh, Honon, could I talk with you privately?"

"What about?"

"That new boy, Mercer."

Peter and Honon exchanged glances, but it was impossible for Peter to tell what was going on in the leader's mind. "Whatever you're going to say about him can be said in public," Honon stated.

Harvey was clearly embarrassed by what he had to say, but equally determined to get it out. "Did you know that he's a . . . a . . . homosexual?"

"Yes. Who told you?"

"The Russian."

Honon grimaced at that. "And who told him?"

"He said it was Marcia."

"And who told her?"

"Apparently Mercer himself. From what I heard, he wasn't trying to hide it or anything."

"Good. I don't think it's healthy for anyone in as small a group as ours to keep personal secrets."

"But what are we going to do about him?"

"I don't know. It's obvious that you have a few suggestions, so why don't you enlighten me?"

Harvey hesitated, shifting his weight from one foot to the other. "Well, I don't mean to sound like a bigot or anything, but I don't think he should be allowed to come with us."

"I'm glad you don't *mean* to sound like a bigot," Honon growled under his breath. A little louder he asked, "Why not?"

"Well, he's . . . he's not our type. We wouldn't get along with him and he wouldn't get along with us. I think he'd be happier on his own."

"The point is, does *he* think he'd be happier on his own? Have you taken the trouble to ask him?"

"No," Harvey said slowly. "I thought you should. . . ."

"You thought I should bell the cat, is that right?"

"Well, you brought him here!"

Honon was about to make a crisp retort, then thought better of it. Instead, he said in lowered tones, "Harv, do you feel threatened by him?"

"Me? No! I . . . I was only thinking about the good of the caravan."

The big man thought on that for a moment, then gave a private wink to Peter. "You're right, Harv. The good of the caravan." Suddenly he bellowed out in a voice that could be heard all the way down the line of cars. "General Council Meeting. I want all adults assembled in five minutes in front of the lead truck."

Turning to Peter, he added privately, "Now we'll see exactly what the 'good of the caravan' is."

CHAPTER 6

Americans have had a taste of what a relative handful of independent truckers can do to this country's living and working habits.

When the independents quit rolling in early February in protest against skyrocketing prices and short supplies of diesel fuel—

• Violence flared on the nation's highways. . . .

• Gasoline supplies, woefully short already in some places, were reduced to critical levels. . . .

• Stocks of meat and other perishable foods dwindled in retail stores, bringing on a wave of panic buying. . . .

• As many as 100,000 workers were idled. Food-processing plants and the auto industry were especially hard hit. . . .

• Mail service slowed to a near halt . . . Magazine deliveries encountered massive delays. . . .

Many affects were cumulative. Food shortages, particularly, could continue for a while.

—U.S. News & World Report
February 18, 1974

Distribution is the biggest of the Big Three. If we had to we could live without communicating past our local area. We could travel to nearby stores on foot or by bicycle and possibly find a job closer to home. But distribution is the killer. . . .

Close to one-half the population of the Earth currently lives in cities. That figure is much higher for the United States and other developed nations. And cities are totally dependent on outside resources. No city in the world with a population of greater than a couple of thousand people can support itself. That is a fact—a fact which will become increasingly more deadly the longer we wait. . . .

In order to get food from where it is raised to where the people are, we need transportation—something we have already seen is in short supply. To make the transportation efficient, we need communications—and they, too, are being shot to hell. . . .

What good is it for a factory to make radios if there's no way to get the product to the people who want to buy it? How can a shop owner keep his store open when delivery of merchandise is spotty and he can't guarantee what he'll have in stock? How secure will the consumer feel if he has no way of knowing from one day to the next whether he'll be able to buy what he needs?

The futility of overproduction and the breakdown of distribution is what will kill the cities. Agricultural communities won't escape the Collapse, either—they never do—but they'll fare better than most. At least they'll have the food. . . .

—Peter Stone
World Collapse

* * *

The General Council Meeting assembled more or less within the time limit set by Honon, with people straggling in every few minutes. Most of them were perplexed, for there didn't seem to be any immediate threat or need for such a meeting. "Does he have to be here?" Harvey asked, pointing at Lee Mercer.

"Trying him *in absentia* would hardly be democratic would it?" Honon said. "Besides, he's entitled to know what the charges are against him."

He stood up and addressed the group as a whole. "Certain rumors have been flying in the last few hours. They finally nested in my ears, so I thought I ought to call this meeeting for the good of the caravan to discuss the matter once and for all. Harvey, why don't you tell everyone what you told me?"

"Well, uh, it's about the new fellow, Mercer." Harvey's eyes were focused on his shoetops, and his voice was barely audible. "I, uh, have it on reliable authority that he, uh, he's different."

"Say it." Mercer's voice rang out bitterly. "I'm gay."

There were a couple of intakes of breath and a few other nods around the circle as people reacted to this announcement. Honon let it set in a while, then said, "The point of this meeting is to decide whether we should let that fact override our invitation for him to join this group."

"It doesn't bother me any," said Sarah Finkelstein.

"Or me, either," said Marcia. "It'll be one less set of male hands I have to fight off, that's all."

A slight laugh went through the crowd at her remark. When the tittering had subsided, Zhepanin rose angrily to his feet. "Is this a matter to joke about, that we will share our meals and our homes with sexual perverts?"

"Are you afraid I'll rape your women?" Lee asked vehemently. "Or are you more worried about your own fair white body? If it'll make you feel any safer, you can sleep with a cork up your asshole."

"There's more to it than that," the Russian said.

"I'll say there is." That was Risa jumping up and facing the meeting. "There's something called trust. We have to all trust each other if we're going to make it. Here I am, a young, single girl surrounded by a lot of men. Any one of you could probably rape me if you wanted, but that doesn't stop me from going along. I trust you. If Lee is willing to trust us, I don't see why we can't trust him."

"Homosexuality is forbidden in all civilized countries," Zhepanin went on over Risa's objections. "It is unnatural, unwholesome and ungodly. Am I right, Father?"

Jason cleared his throat and spoke slowly. "I'm not so sure the lines are cut as clearly as that. Remember, I'm from San Francisco; the last census I saw said that the population there was something like twenty percent gay. You become a bit more tolerant in circumstances like that. I've also met a few gay priests, and they seemed like perfectly respectable men to me. I admit that the Bible is somewhat against it. . . ."

Zhepanin beamed a smug smile. "As I said."

"But each generation must reinterpret the Bible in the light of its own experiences. I'm not sure that what God told to a nomadic tribe several thousand years ago is one hundred percent applicable to the complexities of our situation."

Peter allowed himself a tight little grin. That was precisely the message he had tried to get across to the priest that morning; maybe it had sunk in, after all.

The Russian was silent for a moment, then decided to take a new tack. "He will be of no use to the new colony whatsoever. We will need men who can breed, who will help populate the new world. Men who will have children."

Dom Gianelli stood up. "I already have five. That's enough for both of us." The camp broke up in general laughter.

"Oscar Wilde had children," Lee pointed out when the laughter had subsided again. "In fact, many happily married men with large families have been closet gays. If it is my duty to Humanity to marry and reproduce, I will not shirk it. But I must reserve the right to gain my pleasure in my own way."

At this point, Honon stood up. It was the signal to everyone else to be quiet. The big half-breed looked the group over, staring into the eyes of individuals as though trying to read their souls. Finally he spoke. "If Gregor thinks that Lee would be no use to us, I'd like to see him build a city without an architect. We already have several, of course, but the more the better. But more than that, I think Gregor has raised a serious question for us to consider—namely, whether we are going to limit our recruiting. We have to decide just what will be acceptable to us. If homosexuals are out, then what about people with red hair?" He turned sharply to look at the Itsobus. "What about people with yellow skins? Or haven't you all enjoyed the meals Charlie makes? What about Jews? Are Sarah and Marcia and I beginning to get on your nerves? What about blacks? I, for one, would hate to go without Kudjo. Maybe we should get rid of the Catholics, too.

"Once you start this thing, where do you stop? Intolerance is a plague; once it gets established, it ravages the entire community and it's hell to get rid of. We'd have a pretty small caravan left if we started kicking people out because they were different from ourselves. Part of my job, in fact, is to collect people who *are* different; if the human race is to stay alive, we'll need all the different elements that have gone into making us up.

"There are only twenty-five people right now in our group, including the children, so I'd like you to think carefully before voting to start the epidemic of bigotry. If this small a number of people can't work peacefully side by side, then what hope is there for the rest of Humanity? We might as well not go on."

He paused to indicate he had finished his say, then continued, "All right, all those in favor of booting poor Lee out into the desert, signify by saying aye."

A dead silence followed. Honon waited a moment to make sure of the result, then said, "Unanimous vote to retain him. Sometimes I wonder how these arguments get started when there's nobody really against the issue. Okay, we've wasted enough time here. We'll be moving out in half an hour. Kudjo has found us a gas station on the other side of town; we'll be hitting it shortly after dark."

The Council Meeting broke up and people went their separate ways back to their own vehicles, preparing to move out. Several people went over to Lee to congratulate him; only one person, Zhepanin, pointedly ignored him. From the scowl on his face, he was unhappy with the way the meeting had gone, but was not about to challenge Honon openly.

"That 'Council Meeting' was a farce," Peter said to Honon as they walked over to the lead truck. "You knew all along what was going to happen."

"Of course," Honon answered. "No good leader will ever force a vote unless he's sure he'll win."

They drove through Yuma along Interstate 8. There were no lights on in the city, of course, which added to the general feeling that the town was practically deserted. On the eastern side of the city they stopped and conducted a raid on a gas station. Zhepanin was aghast at this "criminal activity" and refused to participate, but Lee's presence more than made up for the loss. The young architect moved with a gracefulness that rivaled even Kudjo's. "A natural-born guerrilla," Honon remarked to Peter behind Lee's back.

The raid was almost identical to the previous one, and Peter could see how the caravan members had gotten the procedure down to a science. Security

91

practices around gas stations in medium-sized communities were designed to prevent theft by street gangs and hooligans; no provision had been made for organized groups who hit quickly and silently, took what they needed and then vanished into the night. With the breakdown of law enforcement agencies, pursuit was nil; none of the locals wanted to waste any of their depleted stocks by chasing after an obviously well-rehearsed gang.

The caravan drove on through the night for several hours, finally coming to a stop outside the town of Casa Grande. The gas supplies were starting to sink again, though not dangerously so, and Honon thought they might be able to fill up here tomorrow night. He appeared to be in no great hurry to get the caravan where it was going, and didn't want to risk going into a strange town in the dark.

The next day went by uneventfully. Peter and Risa, when they weren't resting, spent more time together. The feeling between them was growing deeper the more they got to know one another. "They'll be going steady in a couple of weeks," Marcia remarked good-naturedly.

Zhepanin was also about. He seemed to have a split personality, being bubbly and charming to the children while grumbling to any adult who would listen. Honon, he said, was a bully and a tyrant, motivated solely by the need for personal power. He intimated that Honon enjoyed robbing his way through the countryside, and enlisted members to his band by appealing to their idealism.

These rumors eventually filtered back to Peter, who confronted Honon with them. The big man sighed and shrugged his shoulders philosophically. "I had a harder time talking him into coming along than anyone else I can remember; it took me all day. He's a very argumentative sort. But we need him, Peter; that starship has to be propelled by nuclear systems and he's the best man to develop and handle them. So we try to put up with him, shortcomings and all. Fortunately, this trip won't last forever."

"Are we nearly there?"

There was a gleam in Honon's eye. "That would be telling. Remember, that question isn't kosher."

With sundown, the caravan began moving again. Casa Grande turned out to be dry of gasoline, so the decision was made to travel on to Tucson. Risa, in particular, was thrilled by that news, since she might now have the chance to see her mother once again.

The party rejoined their old friend, Interstate 10, and began moving in a southeasterly direction towards Tucson. They drove at a leisurely pace, because they didn't have much distance to travel tonight. Honon wanted to stop just outside Tucson so that Kudjo could scout the area tomorrow and find an available gas station.

When they were twenty-five miles outside of town, Honon suddenly slammed on the brakes. There, lined up across the highway in an obviously intentional formation, was a roadblock of old cars. The line was three cars wide and covered all lanes of the road. On pure reflex, Honon grabbed the walkie-talkie suspended under the dashboard. "General alert!" he called to all cars. "Close ranks in a hurry and turn off your lights. Get the children on the floor, pronto. Adults are to grab their guns, roll down their windows and be prepared for action. Await further orders."

Within seconds the caravan was in a compact line and the desert was pitch black once more. Even the moonlight was obscured by a layer of dark clouds. Honon glanced over to make sure that Peter had his .38 ready, then grabbed the automatic rifle he kept beside his seat. "What. . . ." Peter began, but Honon cut him off with an abrupt *shush*. He was listening for sounds out in the desert and had no time for talking. Peter listened, too, but could hear nothing.

The silence weighed on him. One minute elapsed, then two, then five. Peter heard tiny noises that might have been small nocturnal animals scurrying about their normal business, but nothing else. He was about to turn to Honon and ask what he was supposed to be listening for when the big man picked up the walkie-talkie again and spoke into it softly. "When I give the word," he said, "I want all lights on again, instantly; then you can commence firing at will. Remember, prepare your eyes for sudden light."

Then more silence, an agonizing fifteen seconds. Finally Honon whispered, "Get ready. . . NOW!"

The two armored trucks, in addition to their headlights, had powerful search beams mounted on their roofs, pointed in all four directions. These came on as well as the front lights, illuminating the landscape for a radius of three hundred feet around. And what Peter saw in that landscape made him gasp with astonishment.

His first impression was that an army was converging on the caravan from out of the desert. On later hindsight he realized that their number could not have been more than twenty-five or thirty, but they looked legion at his first glance. All of them were dressed in black and had blackened out their faces, and all were armed with what appeared to be military-issue weapons.

The lights caught them by surprise and they froze. The spotlights shone directly into their eyes, blinding them momentarily. And that moment was all that was needed. "Open fire!" Honon shouted into the walkie-talkie—needlessly, for the firing began even before the first syllable had left his mouth.

The attackers stunned and blinded were cut down by the gunfire from the line of cars. Peter's eyes took a second to adjust to the light, but his recovery time was naturally faster than that of the men outside—he had been expecting it, and the light was not shining directly into his eyes. He remembered to hold his .38 the way Honon had shown him, right arm stiff with the left hand bracing his right wrist. Sighting along the barrel he squeezed the trigger and felt a massive recoil along his arm—a lot stronger than he'd thought it would be. That shot went wide of its mark, as did the next several. On his fourth shot, however, he managed to hit a man in the leg. As the fellow hit the ground Peter tried two more shots at him, both misses.

Beside him, Honon's rifle was barking with authority. The caravan leader was taking his time and making his shots count; with almost every squeeze of the trigger, another attacker fell.

"I'm out of ammo," Peter said.

Honon didn't take his eyes off the scene outside.

95

"I put a box under your seat," was all the advice he gave, leaving it up to Peter to unravel the mysteries of reloading the .38 by himself.

After several seconds, the men outside recovered from their initial surprise and began moving again. The ones who were still alive dashed for what little cover was available out on the open desert, many of them taking refuge behind the barricade of old cars across the highway. Peter, on a quick scan of the battlefield, counted eleven bodies that were no longer capable of running for cover.

The attackers were firing back now with a vengeance. A hail of bullets raked the side of Peter's vehicle, and he breathed a sigh of relief that it was armored. He kept his head low, under the window level, while he continued puzzling out how to reload his revolver. Suddenly there was the sound of shattering glass and the light outside dimmed—one of the searchlights had been shot out. Without the element of surprise, those spots made excellent targets. Honon moved quickly to turn them off, but before he could a tinkling of glass signaled the loss of a second. "All lights out," he called into the walkie-talkie. "They can see where we are now."

The desert went dark again.

"Damn bandits," Honon growled to Peter. "I knew this trip had been going too quietly. Now we're in for a war of nerves. If we can hang on till dawn we'll make it; those bastards'll scatter in daylight. But in the meantime we're sitting ducks out here."

"Why don't we just back off down the road a bit and wait for morning?"

"I thought of that. I'd love to, but I don't think it'd work. We'd have to go several miles before they'd stop following us—and besides, every mile back we go means twice that amount of gas we'll be using. We're low as it is, and we're gambling that we'll find enough in Tucson. No, I think we'll have to stick it out here and hope that they're too disorganized to throw another major attack against us. We got close to half their people; they may be smarting. I just hope they don't have reinforcements somewhere."

He picked up his walkie-talkie again. "All cars. It looks like we may be in for a long night. The children are to stay down, no matter what—even if they have to mess in their pants. Nobody leaves the cars. The adults in each car are to work out their own shifts; I don't want anyone awake for the entire night, it's bad for the nerves. Sleep one shift and stand guard one shift, as often as needed. If you feel the slightest bit sleepy, wake the person with you and take a nap immediately. I don't want to lose any cars because of drowsiness. Keep your eyes and ears wide open, and shoot at the slightest suspicion. We've got plenty of ammunition along, and it's better to gun down an innocent jackrabbit than to let yourselves get killed by a bandit. Over and out."

They sat in the darkness for awhile as Peter continued trying to load his gun. Finally Honon spotted his problem, took the revolver and showed him how to break it open and reload the chambers. As usual, he made it look easy. Then he said, "You get some rest. I'll stand first watch."

Peter was not about to argue with him; his eyes were so strained from peering out into the darkness

97

that he doubted he'd be able to see anything anyway. Leaving the .38 on the dashboard within easy reach, he curled up and tried to sleep as best he could.

He was awakened about an hour later by the sound of the walkie-talkie coming to life. "Honon," came Kudjo's voice, "I'm sick of this noise. I'm goin' out to stretch my legs."

Honon knew precisely what he meant. "Okay, but be careful. And don't get shot by any of our people by mistake."

"What's up?" Peter asked.

"Nothing's changed. Kudjo wants to go out reconnoitering and maybe increase our odds by decreasing their numbers. He never did like sitting around."

Peter stretched and yawned. "I'm feeling a little better now, if you'd like to take a bit of rest."

"Sounds okay, but wake me if anything happens." He was asleep almost immediately.

His hand sweating on the gun handle, Peter peered out into the blackness. The night was a heavy dark curtain that intruded between the world and his senses, shutting out experience and leaving him alone with his thoughts. Occasionally a shot would ring out from one of the cars behind him as one of the caravan members detected something worth shooting at. Occasionally, too, a shot would come from out of the darkness directed at the caravan; apparently the bandits wanted to keep their victims from feeling too secure.

A sound came from outside his window and Peter, after taking just a second to get into position, fired. There was no cry of pain, so if it had been a person,

Peter missed him. The sound did not repeat itself, so Peter chalked it up to nothing more than nerves.

The shot, though, brought Honon instantly awake. "Anything happen?" he asked.

"Thought I heard something," Peter replied, a little embarrassed about having wasted his shot.

"Don't worry about it. It's better that they think we're trigger-happy—it'll keep them from coming too close."

The night dragged on, hour after tense hour. *How come tonight of all nights is twenty hours long?* Peter wondered, but according to Honon's watch it was only three a.m. Sporadic shooting was the only sound that marred the stillness of the desert air. Finally, at three thirty, the walkie-talkie crackled to life. "I got seven of them," came Kudjo's voice. "There's only a handful left. By dawn they'll realize that and scatter."

"Good work," Honon said, clicking off.

The thought that there was only a small number of the enemy left buoyed Peter's spirits somewhat, but did not stop the remaining two hours until dawn from limping along. Vigil could not be relaxed—after all, it took only one man to kill you. Peter and Honon continued to take turns on watch.

At long last, dawn began peeking over the eastern horizon. Silhouetted against the lightening sky were the figures of several men running off into the distance. "It looks like we've chased them," Honon announced to the other cars via walkie-talkie. A cheer went up all the way along the line as the big man added, "Now how about some breakfast? I'm starving!"

CHAPTER 7

"The traditional American view of the pet dog as a benign companion is undergoing a change," says Dr. Bruce Max Feldmann, director of the pet clinic at the University of California at Berkeley. . . .

Feldmann said in an interview that the problem stems from the fact that an increasing number of the nation's 40 million pet dogs are becoming "free-roaming dogs" whose owners let them run wild or no longer want them. "Some people are so alienated that they identify with their dogs and want to give them the kind of freedom they'd like to have but can't," he said.

"More than 40 diseases in the United States can be transmitted from dog to man," Feldmann said. "And there's been a rise in the number of dog bites. More than one million dog bites are reported annually and at least as many go unreported. And there are increasing reports of a new menace—the free-roaming dog pack.

"Pet fecal litter also is unesthetic and a nuisance

as well as a public health hazard," he said. "For example, the 500,000 owned dogs in New York City deposit about 150,000 pounds of feces and 90,000 gallons of urine each day on the streets."

—*Los Angeles Times*
September 20, 1974

Civilized man is spending a fortune to preserve, protect and defend his domesticated pets. Providing the creature comforts for our millions of household friends is a multibillion-dollar industry. In just a couple of years, the system that supports this luxury will break down. Wild packs of dogs will roam the streets at will, terrorizing pedestrians and producing serious health hazards. The cats as is their wont, will be more discreet, scavenging at night from garbage piles, stealing food where they can and breeding ungodly numbers of litters several times a year. The pet population problem is more severe even than ours. We, at least, can operate independently to get food for ourselves; they have been bred completely as slaves, dependent on our largesse. . . .

This is not to say that we should kill off all our pets immediately, for they can serve a useful purpose. Dog, cat and even rat (when raised in a disease-free environment) are all quite edible. . . .

—Peter Stone
World Collapse

*   *   *

The battlefield was not a pretty sight. Nineteen bodies were scattered about the ground, all quite

101

dead. Their clothing was of such a miscellaneous assortment that Honon estimated they must have been robbing passing cars for quite some time to have amassed that collection. Some of the bodies had had their weapons removed by their surviving companions, while others remained intact. Their weapons—U.S. Army issue—were confiscated for the caravan's own arsenal.

"I figure they were mainly Army deserters trying to make their way as freebooters," Honon said. There had been mass desertions from the armed forces four years ago, effectively ending all power that the federal government could wield. "I've seen them in bands like this before around the country. A lot of them don't know anything more than what they were trained to do—kill and plunder. In this world, those are survival traits."

Honon used the children as lookouts to make sure the remaining bandits wouldn't try a surprise daylight attack. He would have left the corpses to the buzzards, who had already begun to pick at the flesh, had not Jason intervened and insisted on giving the men Christian burials. A grave detail was organized, and most of the morning was spent digging a hole for the dead men. Their bodies were dumped in the common grave and Jason said a generalized prayer for their souls.

Miraculously, the members of the caravan had sustained no serious injuries. Gina Gianelli's forehead had been grazed by a bullet; Bill Lavochek had taken a slug in the upper part of his left arm; and four-year-old Joseph Parks had sprained his shoulder when his mother had thrown him onto the floor of the car. Other than that, everyone was unscathed, a fact that astonished Sarah Finkelstein.

Right after the short funeral, Risa went over to Honon and talked to him in low tones. The leader kept shaking his head, but Risa refused to take no for an answer. Finally Honon called Peter over to the discussion. "Peter, maybe you can talk some sense into this lady's head."

"What's the matter?"

"As long as we're stopped here for the day anyway, I'd like to go into Tucson and see if I can find my mother," Risa said. "She's still living here."

"And I keep telling her it's too dangerous," Honon added. "We already know there are bandits in the area; where there's one band there may be more. If she'd asked me earlier I could have sent her out with Kudjo, but he's off now looking for a gas station. I simply don't think it's worth the risk."

Risa looked up at Peter with deep blue eyes. "Please talk him into it. It means so much to me."

"What if I went with her?" he asked Honon.

"Do you think the idea of losing two people is better than the idea of losing one? Not to mention the loss of a motorcycle."

"We can use the motorcycle we took from the cop in L.A.," Peter argued. "And you won't lose us, I promise. I'm a devout coward, and I usually run away from trouble. I'll keep us safe."

"Please," Risa begged.

Honon looked at her for a moment, then turned away. "Okay. Dammit, I never could resist blondes.

But you'd better both be back here by sundown, or we'll leave without you."

Peter and Risa took the motorcycle out of the back of the lead truck and, with a goodbye wave to their friends, set off down the road. Risa was on the back, clinging tightly to Peter; somehow he found the sensation pleasant and exciting. The breeze whipped their hair around. Occasionally, Risa would lean forward and kiss the back of his neck. The day felt so good that Peter could almost divorce himself from time and space and believe that he and Risa were just two people out for a lark on a sunny afternoon. He suddenly felt himself very close to this strange blonde sylph with her tender concern for Humanity and her unabashed idealism.

After riding for thirty minutes they came to the outer suburbs of Tucson. Risa, who had lived here with her mother for several years after her father's death, gave Peter directions on how to get to her house. "I think it might be best if we ditched the cycle somewhere and went in on foot," Peter told her. "We'll attract less attention that way. Also, if someone should find us, we won't have anything with us worth stealing."

Risa agreed with his line of reasoning and directed him to a shopping center where she thought they might be able to stash their vehicle.

Peter had seen several ghost towns in his travels, but never any as desolate as this. He had been traveling mainly down the coast of California; even a deserted town there held some semblance of life. Tucson was dead in most senses of the word.

Shopping centers these days were normally guarded by the community because their stores held irreplaceable merchandise, but this one was barren of people, a skeleton without benefit of flesh. Every store window had been broken at one time or another, with no efforts to patch them up. Each shop had been raped—stripped bare, invaded, despoiled, abandoned. Obscene slogans were spraypainted on the walls of buildings, as well as braggadocio by what appeared to be rival juvenile gangs. Loose bits of paper and scraps of cloth blew around in a mild desert breeze, which also lifted the layer of dust and carried it through the air, giving the scene the tone of a realistic painting done in muted colors.

Risa stared around her. Sights she had seen elsewhere had not made their full impact on her because she had not known them when they were alive and vibrant. This was different. She had grown up here, had seen this shopping center filled with people, moving about, laughing, talking, living. Now it was all still—all that moved was trash before the wind. "What . . . what happened?" she whispered.

Peter put his hands gently on her shoulders. "The people moved away."

"But . . . but people have left other towns we've visited and none of them has looked so . . . dead." Her eyes turned upwards toward his, begging for an explanation.

"We haven't stopped in any real desert communities before. You have to realize just how utterly dependent these places are on the outside world. Coastal, agricultural or mountain areas are much better situated to survive a blow like this. The desert has always been a precarious environment. When things started going bad, the people must have moved out in droves."

Risa gulped, took one final look around and said, "Let's go. This place is making me nervous."

They parked their motorcycle in a walkway between two deserted stores, behind some overturned garbage cans. From more than a couple feet away the cycle was invisible, so they assumed it would be safe enough there. They began walking.

As they progressed, it became clear to Peter that all they would see was more of the same. There were some people still living here—that much was obvious from the piles of new garbage and attempts to start gardens in front lawns. More often than not, the gardens looked sickly and desperately in need of watering. Occasionally they caught glimpses of people peering at them through Venetian blinds, but no one came out to talk to them and they met no one else on the streets.

Risa was making a deliberate effort to ignore the dismalness of her surroundings. She walked along at a brisk pace, forcing Peter to hurry to stay with her, and kept up a nonstop stream of verbiage to occupy her mind. She related all sorts of trivial anecdotes about her life here to cover her growing concern about her mother's safety.

"There's the high school I went to. I didn't do too well in the academic subjects; that's why I dropped out after a year. The only thing I was really interested in was arts and crafts. Mrs. Berman, my

Art teacher, said I had a natural gift, and I guess she was right. I went steady for a while, just before I left and moved to Monterey. His name was George Williams, and he was leader of the debating team. I guess I was attracted to intellectuals even then. . . ."

"Quiet!" Peter warned suddenly. He pulled her back into the shadow of a deserted house and pointed off to their right. A group of twelve young men was sauntering down the other side of the street as though they owned the neighborhood. They all wore blue-jean jackets and faded denim flared pants; their shiny leather cowboy boots made sharp clicking sounds on the pavement as they walked. They took their time going down the street, checking garbage cans and peering in windows. They kept up a stream of chatter among themselves, laughing and making obscene jokes that weren't funny. Occasionally, one of them would throw a rock against a house or a fence just to see the damage it would do.

They hadn't noticed Peter and Risa yet. The two from the caravan pressed themselves against the wall as tightly as they could, hoping that the shadows would keep them inconspicuous. The youths, though, seemed more intent on exploring the other side of the street and gave hardly a glance in their direction. Within fifteen minutes they had passed out of sight around a corner, and Peter and Risa began breathing easier again.

"Scavengers," Peter said. "Picking at the bones of a dead city just like the vultures we had to chase away from those bodies this morning."

"I knew two of them," Risa said. "I went to school

107

with them. One of them was in my English class."

Peter shook his head. "That was worlds ago, I'm afraid. The two of you no longer inhabit the same universe."

"I suppose you're right." She looked down at her feet. "Why did all this have to happen, anyway?"

The began walking again. "It's part of the natural system of checks and balances," Peter said. "There was once an area where ranchers killed off all the coyotes that were menacing their sheep. The coyotes had also been keeping the deer population in line, though, and once they were gone the deer began breeding out of control. In just a couple of years, the deer population was so high that there wasn't enough food for all of them. They starved in large numbers, and only a few survived.

"The same thing happened to us. As long as our own coyotes—war, famine, disease—kept us in line, things proceeded smoothly enough. But then we eliminated the coyotes without making compensations in our population or in our governmental and economic systems. We ate ourselves out of house and home, and now we're paying the penalty."

"But does it always have to be this way, going from feast to famine and back again?"

"Not if we learn from our mistakes. The trouble is that we seldom do. If we could learn to plan our future instead of just letting it happen to us we might be able to muddle through. That's why the idea of the Monastery and the colony on Epsilon Eridani interests me—it sounds as though someone is trying hard to set up a planned society. I tried to get people to start one before the Collapse, but they would have been working on too big a scale. This is the sort of thing that has to be done on a small group at first, then built up gradually."

She did not answer, but kept her eyes straight ahead. Peter knew she was having to confront the basic optimism of her nature, and he did not press any harder.

There was a yapping down the street and, a few seconds later, a pack of dogs came into view. There were twenty of them, of nearly as many different breeds. A big Doberman led them along the center of the street at an easy trot.

Once again they retreated from the sidewalk to take shelter in the shade of a deserted house. "More scavengers," Peter muttered. "No wonder people are afraid to leave their houses much, with mongrel hordes—human and canine—wandering loose. It must be hell after dark."

The leader of the pack stopped in front of them and sniffed the air. Peter and Risa caught their breath. The dog looked in both directions, then began jogging over towards them to investigate their odor. Peter had his .38, but didn't dare use it— the noise of the shot might bring the human scavengers back in this direction, and that was something he did *not* want. In desperation, he picked up a rock and threw it at the Doberman. The missile hit the dog's flank, making it yelp in pain and surprise. It stopped, as if deciding whether to fight or flee, and finally decided on the latter course. Nighttime was a dog's proper element; had it been dark, Peter would have had a battle on his hands.

When the dog pack had left, the two humans came out of hiding and proceeded on their way once more. "It's only about another block," Risa said, her spirits lifting once more as she came into familiar territory. She began moving faster, as though her old home were a magnet drawing her ever more strongly the closer she came.

They rounded the corner and her excitement grew. "There it is!" she cried. "Third from the end, with the yellow mailbox painted with flowers." She was running for it, now, with Peter walking quickly after her.

The house was undistinguished except for its oddly decorated mailbox—a tract home in the psuedo-Spanish style so popular in the Southwest. Yellow stucco covered the walls and a high stone arch served as the gateway to the front porch. The roof was of red tiles, looking somewhat the worse for wear.

Even as he approached, Peter could tell that the house was deserted. It had a dry, desolate look about it, from the unkempt lawn to the windows that were caked with dirt. The signs were obvious, but Risa was ignoring them. "Mama, mama," she shouted, running up the front steps. "I'm home!"

She pushed at the front door and it swung open easily, slamming against the inside wall. Before Peter could get to her she had run inside. There was nothing he could do but follow.

He found her standing in the center of the living room, staring around her in disbelief. The room was a little too bare to have been this way normally; some of the furniture must have been taken out. What was left had been casually destroyed.

A vase lay shattered on the floor where it had fallen. A table with one leg cracked leaned perilously against the far wall. The lamp that had stood upon it was on the ground next to it. The shade had been crushed on one side; the cord was still in the electrical outlet. One faded easy chair squatted in a corner to Peter's left, its pillow sliced open and the stuffing scattered about the room. There was a thick layer of dust on the windowsills.

"But . . . it's only been two years, maybe a little more," Risa was saying quietly, more to herself than to him. "What happened?"

"Risa." He took a step towards her, arms outstretched to comfort her, but she moved away from him.

"Mama?" she said, more hesitantly this time, as she walked zombie-like into the kitchen. She emerged after a minute and clumped listlessly into the back room area. The footsteps stopped. Then suddenly she screamed.

Peter ran after her. The layout of the house was unfamiliar to him, but after finding one bedroom and a bathroom unoccupied, he came to the room she was in. He found her lying on the floor in a heap, sobbing uncontrollably, and he knelt beside her.

Cradling her head in his hands, he asked, "What happened?"

In answer, she pointed at the wall on their left. A large red smear stained the wall's white paint, and little rivulets of red had run down the wall from the site of the smear to the floor. The stains were quite dry by this time. There was no body or anything on the floor to indicate what had happened here.

"She's dead," Risa cried. "They've killed her."

Peter held her sobbing body closely against his own. His hands gently stroked her back as he tried to comfort her. "We don't know that."

"That's her blood."

"How can you tell? It could just as easily be someone else's blood. It . . . it could be a dog's blood, for all we know. Anything could have happened."

"But she's not here. . . ."

"Maybe she moved out to San Francisco. Maybe one of those gangs of kids moved in and had a fight in here. Maybe . . . I don't know, maybe any one of a million things. There's no body here, so how can we know? Why should you want to assume the worst?"

With an effort of will, Risa stopped her crying. She sat up straight and sniffled back a few remaining tears. "Mama always said she didn't want to move ever again." Her voice had a strange, far-away quality to it. "She always said she wanted to die right here when her time came."

"Times change. People change."

Risa was not listening. Slowly she pushed Peter away from her, got to her feet and walked out of the room. There was definitely something odd about her. Her air of innocence and youth had evaporated.

She walked stiffly, as though no longer entirely a part of the real world. *Something's died inside her,* Peter realized. *The lid's been blown off her naivete and she can't maintain the facade of idealism anymore.* He mourned the death of her innocence with more genuine grief than he had felt in years.

He did not go after her immediately. It would be better to leave her alone with her thoughts for awhile, to let them simmer and sink to their natural level. He sat down on the carpeted floor of the bedroom, immersed in his own private thoughts of the world, the caravan, the colony, the Monastery.

An hour later he got up and went to search for her. She wasn't in the bathroom or the other bedroom. He went out into the living room, and she wasn't there, either. He began to worry. Checking the kitchen, he found it a clutter of battered, dirty pans that had been pulled from the cupboards and scattered about the room. Broken china littered the floor. A back door stood slightly ajar; he went through it and there, in the yard, he found Risa.

She was sitting cross-legged on the ground beside an empty concrete hollow that had once been a small frog pond. A withering fern drooped listlessly beside her, and the light breeze blew strands of hair haphazardly into her face. She sat still as a statue, staring across the yard with unseeing eyes.

She must have heard him coming but didn't look up at his approach. "I know how dreams die," she said.

"Risa," he began, but she cut him off.

"They're really very fragile, like soap bubbles.

113

They can be quite beautiful, floating in the air in front of you, but when you reach out to touch them they pop."

He put a hand on her shoulder. She did not resist, but neither did she accept. Her body and her voice were wooden. "You were telling me the other day how your dreams died gradually. I remember thinking at the time how sad that was, and how I hoped it would never happen to me. I thought my world was safe and snug. Now I see it can turn upside-down in a second."

What can you say to someone whose universe has just collapsed? Peter wondered. *What could anyone have said to me when the pieces of the nightmare began forming in my mind? There's no salve for this kind of injury; we can only lick the wound and wait for it to heal over. We wait until the scars become a part of ourselves, and then we go on living. But we can never be the same again.*

"Risa," he said quietly, "It's getting late. I think we'd better start heading back."

"What does it matter?"

"You told me a couple of days ago that you wanted to feel there was still some hope, somewhere, for the world—that we needed dreams as well as facts. There's no hope left here, so we might as well move on to someplace where there is."

"But hopes and dreams can die. . . ."

"Then you go out and look for new ones. But you don't just sit down and give up, or you might as well not have been born. Come on, the caravan needs you. There are people back there who are your friends, who care about you a great deal. I . . . I care about you a great deal, myself." His mouth was suddenly dry. "I love you, Risa."

She looked straight into his face. There was a dead look about her eyes. "A couple of hours ago that would have made me so happy. Now. . . ." She shrugged. "I don't know if I'll ever love anything again. It hurts too much when you lose it."

"Come on." He lifted her to her feet; she arose without protest or enthusiasm. "You'll feel better in a couple of days, once the shock wears off."

"But to think I'll never know what happened to her. . . ."

He put an arm around her waist. "Life is full of unknowns and mysteries. Whenever you say good-bye to someone, there's always the possibility it'll be the last time. Living is changing; old faces go, new ones come. You have to accept it for the chaos it is."

She did not answer as he guided her through the back door of the house and past the mess in the kitchen. Her eyes were focused straight ahead, unseeing, as they went through the living room again and out the front door for the last time. It was as though the house no longer existed for her, as though it had been erased from her memory. It belonged to a past that was now dead.

As they stepped off the porch into the driveway a shot rang out and something whizzed past Peter's ear. Instinctively he jumped back, pulling Risa with him. Across the street, an older man stood in front of his house, aiming a rifle at them. "Let's get out of

115

here," Peter said. Crouching low, he pushed Risa ahead of him; her reflexes caught up with the situation and she began to run, too. Another shot flew by over their heads. Peter risked a look back and saw that the man had put up his rifle and was watching them leave, a scowl on his face. "Damned burglars!" he shouted after them.

Peter and Risa kept running.

CHAPTER 8

Consumer prices in the non-Communist industrialized countries rose by an average of 13.5% in the year ending Aug. 31, the Organization for Economic Cooperation and Development reported Thursday. . . .

Among the OECD members, Iceland had by far the highest inflation rate with a 41.1% average . . . Four other countries—Greece, Turkey, Portugal and Japan—had inflation rates just over 25%. . . .

In all countries, inflation was running two to three times as high as the average increase in the 10 years prior to 1971.

The annual rate in the United States was 11.2%; in Canada, 10.8%, and in Australia, 14.4%.

Rates in other European countries were France, 14.5%; Italy 20.4%; Britain 16.9%; Belgium 14.6%; Denmark 16%; Ireland 17.9%; Finland 16½%; Spain 15.3%; and Switzerland, 10.5%.

—*Los Angeles Times*
Friday October 11, 1974

We are living on the broad, flat top of an inverted paper pyramid. The paper is the currency we exchange every day for the things we buy and the work we do. The paper is the reports that flow between branches of government to give them the appearance of animation. The paper is the computer readouts that depersonalize our lives. . . .

If we chose to label the top of the pyramid "price," then the single shaky stone on which it all rests could be called "worth." If the top is labeled "output," then the bottom is "fact."

Whatever the reasons—and I assure you they are myriad—the complexities of daily living have been inflated beyond the assumptions they're based on. Civilization developed by broadening itself out over the foundation on which it was built— and like a pyramid standing on its head, all it will take is one slight puff of air to send us toppling down. . . .

—Peter Stone
World Collapse

*　　　*　　　*

Peter and Risa returned to the caravan just as the sun was setting, having evaded another pack of wild dogs in getting back to their motorcycle. Dinner was almost over, and Honon greeted their arrival with little more than a grunt. They ate quickly, all the while bombarded with questions from the other members about what Tucson had been like. Peter gave them a short, depressing description of the conditions and mentioned only that Risa's mother had

118

not been there. Risa ate apathetically and said nothing.

After dinner the caravan moved out. Kudjo had found a gas station for them in the center of town, and during the afternoon the caravan members had pushed the barricade of cars off the road, so there was nothing to stop them from continuing on.

The gas station raid was now a routine to Peter, accomplished quickly and without incident. As the procession of cars moved out into open country once more, he settled back in his seat and fell into a contemplative mood. Risa's disillusionment had hit him deeply as well, making him recall the trauma he had undergone just before writing his book. She would survive it, he knew, but whether she would still be the same girl he had come to love was another question.

Honon, sensing the withdrawal in Peter's manner, concentrated on driving and did not bother him with conversation.

Little handpainted signs flashed past along the side of the road: INDIAN TURQUOISE—BARGAIN PRICES; or NAZI WAR MEDALS ON DISPLAY; or REAL INDIAN MUMMY; or GAS! COLD LEMONADE, BEER! They were the lead-in signs to one of the small gas stations/souvenir shops/ museums that dotted the highways of the Southwest. The caravan had already passed several and Honon and Peter paid no attention until a reddish glow appeared on the horizon. "Looks like a fire up ahead," Honon remarked, speeding up to investigate.

It was indeed a fire, and as they approached they could see that the flames were sprouting from a small wooden building which could only be the desert museum heralded by the signs. The building was one story high and could not have contained more than three rooms. The fire must have started just recently, because little of the structure had been damaged yet and some of the faded handpainted lettering could still be seen peeling from the walls.

Honon and Peter got quickly out of the cab and ran to the front of the store. The flames were starting to grow now, preventing them from coming too close, but they were able to gaze in through the window. By the light of the fire they could see the crumpled body of a man lying in the center of the floor.

Braving the heat, Honon climbed onto the front porch and reached for the knob. The metal was hot, and he pulled his hand away quickly. He took a step back, then crashed his full weight against the old wooden door, which gave a satisfying crunch. After a second blow it broke open completely and Honon's momentum carried him stumbling inside, banging into a wooden counter. Through the window Peter could see Honon coughing as he passed through a turnstile, knelt beside the unconscious form and slung it over his shoulder. Bent over from the weight, he carried it out of the burning building just as the ceiling timbers started to collapse. Less than a minute after Honon and the victim had emerged from the doorway the ceiling caved in completely. Burning beams fell to the floor, scattering sparks in all directions.

Honon carried the man thirty feet from the burning building and set him gently down on the ground. Putting his arm under the man's shoulders and tilting the head back slightly, he began mouth-to-mouth resuscitation. It took only a couple of quick breaths before the man's chest was rising and falling on its own.

Now that events were less hurried, Peter took a better look at the victim. He was old, easily into his seventies to judge by the lines in his face, yet his hair and full beard were still mostly black with only a few streaks of gray. The checkered shirt and loose-fitting pants he wore seemed a throwback to the era of hardbitten desert prospectors.

Satisfied that the man was breathing naturally again, Honon backed off and let Sarah Finkelstein, who had rushed up with her black bag, take over. Several of the other caravan members came to stare, but Honon shooed them away to a respectable distance, giving the doctor room to work.

"This man's been beaten," Sarah remarked.

Peter looked down at her. "Huh?"

"Well, the fire sure as hell didn't do this." She turned the man's head to give Peter a better look. In the flickering light of the flames, Peter could see that the man's face was a mass of bruises and cuts. The eyes were puffy and there was a small trickle of blood coming out of the nose and mouth.

"Who could have done it?"

"I don't know," Honon growled, "but whoever did it must have set the fire as well. Probably just before we got here."

Sarah had been checking the man's limbs for breaks, but apparently there were none. She was in the process of taking his pulse when his eyes opened. At first they were glazed with shock, but consciousness slowly seeped its way back in. He moved his jaw with great pain, but his throat was too dry to speak. "Would water hurt him?" Honon asked the doctor.

"You can give him a little. It'll make him feel more comfortable, if nothing else. He doesn't appear too badly burned, and the shock may be wearing off. If it weren't for the beating, I'd say he was in pretty good shape."

Honon bellowed for someone to fetch some water, and pretty soon Machi, the five-year-old daughter of Charlie and Helen Itsobu, came trotting up with a canteen. Honon raised the victim's head and put the canteen to his lips. The old man wanted to drink greedily, but Honlon only allowed him a couple of swallows before pulling the water away again.

"Thank you, stranger," the old man croaked after another few moments of vain attempts at speech. "Who are you, anyway?"

"Name's Honon. My friends and I were passing by when we noticed your light and thought we'd drop in."

The old man tried to lift his head enough to look at the burning building, but was too weak to manage it. "I'm Sam Moorfield. How's my museum doing?"

"As firewood it's going along quite nicely, I'm afraid. We have no equipment to put it out."

The old man groaned. "I had the ceremonial head-dress worn by Chief Sitting Bull himself. I had a collection of glass eyes, close to fifty of 'em. I had the skin of the largest polecat ever seen in the state of Arizona. And now it's lost, all of it." His eyes filled with tears.

"The glass eyes may survive the fire," Peter said, trying to be as consoling as possible.

Sam Moorfield cheered up a little at that. "They just might, mightn't they? They've come through so much already, to last this long. Some of them are over a hundred years old. A real sight to see they were, I'll tell you."

"I'm sure they were," Peter agreed, trying to sound sincere.

Honon switched subjects abruptly. "Who beat you up?"

The man's face twisted into an expression of hatred. "Who? I'll tell you who. Them murdering bastards from down the road, that's who!"

"We're strangers in these parts and we don't know who you mean."

"The people that run the motel out that way." The old man waved a hand weakly toward the east.

"Why would they want to kill you?"

" 'Cause I been warning people, that's why, telling them to stay away. Cuts into their 'business,' you might say. Listen, have you got any beer? The truck hasn't gone by here in close on a year, now, and I really miss my brew."

"No beer. Would vodka do?"

123

"Reckon so."

"Kudjo," Honon's voice crackled with authority, "a bottle of our finest for the gentleman."

"Yassa, Massah Boss," Kudjo grinned. He went into the back of the second armored truck and, after a moment, emerged with a bottle in his hand.

Peter looked at Honon in surprise. "Why are we carrying alcohol? It seems like a waste of space."

"When money breaks down, alcohol is always a good medium of exchange. That's part of our cash reserves. We couldn't get our hands on any cigarettes, or we'd have brought them along, too." He took the bottle from Kudjo and handed it to Moorfield. "There you go, sir, with our compliments. Why were you warning people about the motel down the road?"

" 'Cause they're killers, that's why. They invite people to stay there free for the night—say they're just lonely for the company—then kill 'em and take their goods. Nothing but cut-throats, that's all they are. If there'd been any law, I'd've called it—but there wasn't. I couldn't do much against 'em by myself—there's five of them and only one of me, and I'm pushing seventy-three come next summer. So I started warning people, only *they* didn't like it." He broke the seal on the bottle, untwisted the top and lifted it to his mouth. After taking a healthy swig, he wiped his mouth with the back of his sleeve and said, "You don't know how good that feels after all this time. I sure am lucky you folks happened along."

Honon's jaw was set; a look of determination had

settled on his face. "How far down the road did you say this motel was?"

"Two miles."

Honon turned to face the rest of the caravan members. "I've got a little mission that is strictly volunteer. There seems to be a rat's nest that requires extermination. It may be a little difficult, but I'll do it myself if I have to. Anyone want to come along?"

A chorus of shouts greeted his announcement, led by Kudjo and Peter. Lee Mercer, Charlie Itsobu, Dom Gianelli and Harvey Parks all wanted to join in the action. Bill Lavochek wanted to go, too, but his arm was still healing from its wound and Sarah forbade him to go.

"All right, then," Honon said. "Sarah, you take care of our friend here. We'll be back in a little while."

"Wait a minute." It was Zhepanin speaking up. "Is this what we are to be—a group of vigilantes, a mob terrorizing the countryside? Stealing gasoline here, killing people there—is this how you preserve Civilization?"

"Why not?" Honon countered. "That's what Civilization was based on, for all the lofty morals it spouted. If there were any procedure for Justice here, I would follow it; but the only justice that exists in that motel depends on who's holding the gun at the moment. And when I go there, *I* intend to be the one with the gun."

"Your self-serving rationalizations sicken me," Zhepanin said.

Honon's voice became a little calmer. "Maybe. I never claimed to be perfect, Gregor. When my sensitivities are outraged I strike out to remove the offense. I am not forcing you to come along on this raid. But I *am* the leader of the caravan. If at any time you feel you cannot abide that fact, you are free to leave and either stay here or go back to your home. But remember—I pass this way but once."

"Where else could I go?" the Russian muttered under his breath as he turned away and stalked down the line of cars.

The volunteers for the raiding party got into the back of the armored truck except for Honon and Kudjo, who sat up front. After a short drive, the vehicle stopped again. Honon and Kudjo got out and opened the back for the others. "Okay, here's the situation," Honon said. "The motel is right over there. I noticed as I drove up that there's a lot of junked cars in back; that supports the old man's claim. There was a light on in the office window, probably a candle; some of them are obviously there. Moorfield said there were five altogether. There weren't any cars parked in the courtyard, so we don't have to worry about innocent bystanders. It's just them and us."

"The motel is laid out in a U shape—two long buildings and a connecting one at the back, with a central courtyard/parking lot. It was too dark to see if there was a swimming pool; if there is, it would be in that central area as well. A warning to the wise among you—falling in could be fatal, so watch it.

"We'll split up like we do for gas stations. Dom,

Harvey and I will hit the front office. Kudjo, I want you to take Charlie, Peter and Lee and spread yourselves out along the interior of the court. I want our troops firmly entrenched before the shooting starts in case all these people are not in the office. The moon's near full, which is probably a good thing; I don't want us shooting any of our own people by mistake, so be extra careful. Any questions?"

There were none, so Honon distributed the weapons. This time, Peter was given a Remington .22 autoloader and a two-sentence description of how to work it. Then Honon gave the order to move out. Peter's group went first. He followed behind Kudjo and Lee, with Charlie behind him. They clung to the shadows as they moved down the road and right up to the opening of the central court. The motel was a wooden, single story affair, one long continuous series of rooms shaped, as Honon had said, into a U. Just inside the entrance was an island, an oval of dirt surrounded by stones. A dessicated palm tree and some drooping plants inhabited the island. Kudjo motioned for Charlie to wait behind the tree and moved on with his other two helpers. He stationed Peter in a doorway while he and Lee went elsewhere.

Peter checked the door behind him. It was locked, so he leaned back against it in comparative safety. The desert's night air was cold as he practiced sighting along the length of the rifle barrel. *I hope this won't take too long,* he thought. *I'm freezing.*

Even though he was expecting it, the sheer suddenness of the attack took him by surprise. One moment the night air had been still, the next it was full of gunshots. Screams came from the front office, cut off abruptly by bullets. The light in the office was quickly doused.

"Only two in here," Honon's voice called out. "That leaves three unaccounted for."

Peter's eyes scanned the rows of doors. Even assuming Moorfield was right about the number of people living here, that still did not mean all five were at home tonight. The party from the caravan could wait here tensely until morning, only to find that the other three had left for greener pastures earlier the previous day.

A quick movement in the darkness put an end to that line of speculation. A man's form raced out of one door across from Peter and down the row to another door. Peter had little time to aim and took just a quick shot. He missed, naturally. Several other people also took shots, but they missed too.

Minutes later, gunfire was returned from the room that the figure had entered. Whoever it was had obviously gone from the room where he happened to be at the time of the attack to the room where he kept his weapons. At the same time, more gunfire came from a room at the end of Peter's side of the U. No others sounded, meaning that either there were only two of the enemy capable to shooting or that the three of them were divided into two groups.

It made little difference, in the long run. Barricaded in their rooms, the enemy could hold out indefinitely against the caravan group. They had a clear view of all approaches to the fronts of the rooms, and could gun down anyone foolish enough to attack. A sneak attack from the rear, going in through the room windows, might work, but the attacking party would certainly suffer a few casualties itself in the attempt.

Fifteen minutes of stalemate proved Peter's theory correct. He stood in his doorway, firing occasional shots to keep the defenders honest while slowly freezing to death himself. *Honon must realize it'll be useless for us to stay here all night,* he thought. *I wonder what he plans to do.*

His mental question was answered as he caught sight of a movement on the roof opposite him. Instinctively he raised his rifle, but then recognized the figure as Kudjo running crouched over on top of the building. He was carrying something that Peter couldn't quite make out. He stopped just over the room that held the sniper across from Peter and lit a match. The small flicker of light revealed that the object was another of the vodka bottles from the caravan's supplies. Kudjo lit a short fuse in the bottle neck, set it down on the roof and ran.

A shot rang out from the sniper's room down the row from Peter. Kudjo straightened up briefly, then fell over backwards off the roof and out of sight behind the motel. Peter gasped. He had came to think of Kudjo as almost invincible over these last few days; he hoped his friend had not been killed.

But he had little time to think of Kudjo's fate before the vodka bottle exploded. The roof of the motel had been exceedingly dry, and caught fire immediately. Flames spread almost the length of

129

the building, sending up clouds of thick, black smoke. Suddenly Peter no longer had to worry about feeling cold.

"Back out," Honon called to his men. "We'll ring the area. When they come out, shoot."

Peter retreated as ordered, keeping as close to the side of the building as he could to avoid getting shot. As soon as he emerged from the court he ran around to the back of the motel where Kudjo had fallen. The black man was lying on the ground, writhing in pain. "Are you all right?" Peter asked, running up to him.

"Sheeyit, it takes more than a bullet to stop Kudjo Wilson," the other said. "He got me in the right thigh, is all. On top of which I think I twisted the ankle when I fell."

Peter examined the leg in question. The bullet had gone in slightly below the right hip and had come out cleanly through the other side. Apparently it had missed the bone completely—a lucky circumstance, all things considered. Bleeding was also minimal, for which Peter was profoundly grateful—it had been years since he'd had any first aid training. It was one of the things he'd always meant to get around to and never had.

"Will you stop gawkin' and get back to help Honon?" Kudjo said testily. "I'll be smooth, man, don't worry."

Reluctantly, Peter let himself be shooed off back to the action. He reported to Honon on Kudjo's condition and the leader nodded. "That man could stroll through an elephant stampede and just get his little toe stepped on. Take up a position over there between Charlie and Harvey and get ready. They won't be able to stay in there too much longer."

As Peter took the indicated post he could see that Honon was right. The desert air had dried the wood of the motel and it burned as though it had been doused in kerosene. Already it was a solid wall of flame, and Peter could hear timbers cracking. Part of the roof fell in, sending up a rain of sparks. The fire, like a sentient being smelling triumph, roared louder.

A figure ran from the burning building. He had dropped his rifle behind him, not wanting it to explode in his hands, and his clothing was on fire. Honon picked him off with one clean shot through the head. Several minutes later another person came running out of the blaze. This man had seen what had happened to his compatriot, and had not dropped his gun. He came out firing—but he was firing at figures in the dark whereas the men from the caravan could see his shape clearly outlined against the fire. He went down quickly in a hail of bullets.

The building had half collapsed when a third figure emerged, this one carrying a white flag on an improvised pole. But it was not the truce symbol that stayed the man's hands at their guns so much as the fact that this figure was that of a young, slender girl.

She walked slowly out of the flames, then collapsed on the ground. Peter, Honon and Lee rushed forward immediately, with the other men right at their heels. The girl could not have been more than sixteen years old, with flowing brown hair and a face of total innocence. She was exceptionally pretty as she lay unconscious at their feet.

"What'll we do with her?" Harvey Parks wondered.

Honon's voice was rock hard. "Kill her."

"What? That sweet thing?"

Honon turned on him with bearlike ferocity. "Yes. Apparently you don't know the way a trap like this works. 'That sweet thing' is the bait that pulls men in, with the implied promise of sex with her. Maybe she even does go to bed with them, I don't know. Then, when the guy's asleep, her friends come in and kill him. She has been responsible for any number of cold-blooded murders. I've seen this thing too many times across the country to let it go on."

"But even so. . . ."

"You're letting the fact that she's a pretty girl influence your thinking, Harv. You're using your gonads instead of your brain."

"Well, she doesn't affect my gonads," said Lee, "and I want to let her live, too."

Honon paused. "Why?"

"She's so young that she's not totally responsible for her actions. Even if she's the bitch goddess of the Western World, she was molded that way by her companions. They're neutralized, now; maybe without them she'll have the chance to go on to better things."

"I refuse to take her on the caravan."

Lee shrugged. "Then leave her here. But leave her alive; at least she'll have a chance."

"A chance to move into Tucson and take up with one of those gangs Peter told us about?" Honon asked—but as he looked around the faces of the men it became evident that Lee spoke for all of them. "Okay, I won't fight you all at once. But I hope you'll be able to sleep nights with your consciences telling you she may be responsible for the deaths of several more people. Come on, let's find Kudjo and get back to the caravan."

Under Honon's direction, they splinted Kudjo's wounded leg and carried him gently over to the truck. After laying him in the back, they all climbed in and began the short drive back to the other vehicles.

Sarah Finkelstein immediately went to work on her new patient and, after a few minutes, announced that he had been incredibly lucky not to have a bone shattered, but that the leg would have to be bound up securely for several weeks. Kudjo groaned at this, but Honon gave him stricts orders to obey the doctor.

Sam Moorfield came over to Honon. "I want to thank you for saving my life and for helping me. I think I'd better be traveling on, now."

"Has Sarah told you about our colony?"

"Yep. Sounds interesting."

"You're a pretty cagey old goat. Would you like to come along? I think you'd make a good addition to our survival teams."

The old man shook his head. "No, that colony of yours is for the young folks. I'm too tired of this old world to start in building a new one. I've lived most of my life in this here desert; figure I might as well die out here, when my time comes."

Honon smiled at him. "Whatever you say. We've got to be shoving off right now." They shook hands. "Take care, Sam."

"You too, Honon."

Though the men had known each other for only a couple of minutes, Peter could definitely sense a feeling of kinship between them, almost like father and son. As the old man walked back to his still-smoldering house, Honon stood and watched him for a moment. Finally he turned and looked at the assembled multitude of the caravan. "What are you all staring at? Get moving—we've still got some traveling to do tonight!"

CHAPTER 9

If present trends continue, according to the U.N.'s latest "Demographic Yearbook," the population of the earth will double by the year 2006—reaching 7.4 billion just 33 years from now. . . .

Actually, the world's birth rate, over all, is on a decline. But so are death rates, as medical research reduces infant mortality, particularly in developing countries, and all but eliminates "killing epidemics." In the majority of countries today, people are living longer. . . .

So explosive is the growth in developing regions that population authorities fear hunger and famine will become even more widespread. Moreover, they warn, the more crowded that living conditions become the greater is the prospect of violence and upheaval. But bigger populations are causing difficulties—pollution, traffic congestion, shortages of resources—in the wealthier, industrialized nations, too. And compounding the problem all over the world is that more and more people are crowding into cities. . . .

—*U.S. News & World Report*
March 12, 1973

The root cause of all the breakdown seems to be people. There are too damn many of them. All our institutions, all our laws, all our procedures for dealing with social interactions have been designed exclusively for small numbers of people living in uncrowded communities. When you overload a circuit, it shorts out, and this is precisely what's happening. . . .

You can't provide justice when the courts are so clogged that it's impossible to keep the cases straight. Police can't enforce the laws fairly when there are too many people to watch over. Administration can't function when of necessity it must be given over to processing the masses instead of judiciously handling each complaint as an individual case. Too many people take up too much space, eat too much food, eliminate too much waste and use up too many irreplaceable resources too quickly. . . .

For thousands of years, a marginal ability to survive meant that having many children was a blessing for families. In a scant two hundred years we have reversed that maxim—but we have neglected to change the institutions that were based on it. The resulting chaos is all around us. . . .

—Peter Stone
World Collapse

*   *   *

Nothing much was said to the people who'd stayed behind about how the raid on the motel had gone; all that was mentioned was that it had been successful. After Sarah had finished bandaging Kudjo, the caravan set off eastward again along Interstate 10. As they passed the spot where the motel was still burning, Peter noted that the body of the young girl was no longer lying where they'd left it; she must have come to and decided to take advantage of her unexpected reprieve. He gave a slight sigh and hoped she would be smart enough to make the most of her opportunity.

The road stretched eastward for mile after boring mile. Traveling in the dark, there was not even a view of the breathtaking desert panorama to make the journey interesting—just that line down the center of the road illuminated by the car's headlights. Occasionally they would pass through a small town, but its existence was made known to them only by the change in the kind of road signs along the side of the highway. Sometime after midnight they crossed over the border from Arizona into New Mexico, but it made little difference—the road was still the same.

At about three-thirty, Honon pulled the vehicle off to the side of the road, and the rest of the cars in the line followed his example. Peter noticed that the gas gauge was reading very low. "We've got a choice now," Honon said, and fatigue was registering in his voice. "There are only two places in this area where we might get gas—Las Cruces and El Paso. El Paso is significantly farther away, but I know a place that's almost sure to have what we need. Las Cruces is just ahead, but it's an unknown quantity. In either case, we'd have to wait till daylight before taking any action—and I sure as hell need the sleep." He picked up the walkie-talkie and called the other cars. "Okay, everybody, we'll be stopping here through breakfast at the least. Let's all bed down and get a good night's sleep."

It seemed as though morning were coming earlier every day. Peter stretched and tried to shake the sleepiness out of his head. This schedule of irregular waking hours and grabbing catnaps at odd intervals was playing havoc with the systems of most of the caravan members. Peter hoped the trip would end soon, before they were all too tired to care whether they got to the Monastery or not.

To make matters worse, Zhepanin approached them as they came up to the camper for breakfast. *Oh no, not on an empty stomach,* Peter thought, but it looked as though there'd be no way to avoid the confrontation.

"I have been talking to Charlie," the Russian began brusquely. "He tells me that we have only enough supplies for one or perhaps two more days. Is that correct?"

Honon paused and thought. "Yeah, that sounds about right."

"What will you propose we do when those supplies run out? Steal the food from the mouths of starving infants?"

"Oh ye of little faith," Honon muttered under his breath. Aloud, he said, "Maybe I plan to call down manna from the heavens."

"I do not think this is a matter for jokes. All along this trip you have proved yourself a freebooter and an adventurer. I do not believe there is such a thing as your 'Monastery' or the interstellar space ship. I suspect this is all a charade you use to entice people into your little band. Once they are far from their homes and friends, they dare not leave you. In this way, you are building yourself up a pirate group that can roam the country at will and take what it wants by force."

Honon listened to Zhepanin's ravings quietly. When the Russian had finished, he said, "A very interesting supposition. But if that were so, why would I be taking people with families? There are lots of stoners these days who would jump at the chance to join a wandering band. And why would I put up with you, a nuclear propulsion engineer, if I didn't have a rocket that needed propelling?"

"Maybe you need me to keep up appearances," Zhepanin shrugged. "Madmen do not need reasons."

"Madmen *always* have reasons. They just don't make sense to rational minds." With that, Honon turned his back on Zhepanin and continued with Peter to the camper.

Peter was thoughtful as they stood in line for food. Zhepanin had raised a good point. There were now twenty-five people in the caravan. Though Charlie was brilliant at making a few supplies go a long way, their stores were rapidly being depleted. As yet, they had made no raids on towns for food—but could that continue? An alternative thought occurred to him: could they be getting so near the Monastery that more supplies would be unnecessary? As he'd thought before, the desert was a great place to hide a large project like this—but where could it be?

Honon and Peter sat down by Lee to eat their breakfast. "I think we'd better try Las Cruces for gas," Honon said. "We're awfully low and we might

139

run out trying for El Paso. I do have a few spare cans full, but I don't like using them.

"Las Cruces, though, raises another problem—reconnaissance. Kudjo is in no shape to go scouting, and I'd rather stay back here and keep an eye on Gregor to make sure he doesn't get too far out of line with his speculations. That leaves the two of you as the men I would most trust to go out and look the town over."

"Sure, I'd be glad to volunteer," Lee said, to which Peter chimed in with, "I'm willing."

"Good. I knew I could count on you. Kudjo will be pleased to learn that it takes two other people to handle his job. You both know the sort of things you're looking for—gas stations with guards around them, roadblocks, any potential hazards along the route. Since we're low on gas, it might be best if you shared one motorcycle; we may need every extra drop."

Lee and Peter nodded. Finishing their breakfasts quickly, they went over to the lead truck and got one of the motorcycles out of the back. "How about if I do the driving?" Lee suggested. "I used to race these things on weekends, before the gas crunch got out of hand."

"Fine with me," said Peter. He strapped on a holster and made sure his .38 was loaded.

As they drove into town, they exchanged small talk on what their respective lives had been like before the Collapse and what they thought the future of Mankind might be like here on Earth. "The Monastery," said Peter, "is an unknown factor. Without it, we might need centuries to even begin to approach

140

the levels we attained before the Collapse. But with it—well, who can say? If it does preserve Man's knowledge and skill it just may shorten that time-span considerably."

The town of Las Cruces was not nearly as desolate as Tucson, which was in keeping with one of Peter's theories. "The magnitude of the Collapse in any particular area," he had written, "will be directly proportional to how built up that area was to begin with." Las Cruces had been a smaller town than Tucson, and so had suffered less—but even it had not emerged unscathed.

The home gardens, of course, were very much in evidence. Here and there were the rotting hulks of cottonwood trees that had been uprooted so that more practical crops could be grown. There were people working in their yards who stared at the cycle as it passed; any functioning motor vehicle was a rarity these days, and aroused people's curiosity.

There were plenty of gas stations, but all of them appeared deserted. Peter and Lee crisscrossed the streets without much success—until they rounded one corner and nearly drove head-on into an angry mob of people.

Lee skidded the motorcycle to a halt and they took in the situation quickly. The mob comprised about fifty white men, most of them brandishing im-provised clubs. Two men at the front were carrying a rope and dragging along with them a young Mexi-can woman. The expression on the men's faces was anger; that on the girl's was pure terror.

"Let's go around the block, quick," Peter said, and Lee jumped to obey. With a squeal of tires the cycle took off in the direction from which it had come. Several rocks were thrown after it as it turned the corner and disappeared from the mob's view, but none of them hit.

"What was that all about?" Lee asked.

"I'd say they're going to lynch that poor girl."

"Why?"

"She's pregnant and she's Latin. Didn't you notice she was about seven months along? A desert community struggling to survive would naturally resent any new mouths to feed—particularly if they belong to a minority group. In case you hadn't noticed, racial tensions are at a new high these days."

Lee's face hardened. "We've got to save her."

"I agree. But we can't face down a mob of fifty men by ourselves. We'll need help."

"She'd be dead before we could get back here with reinforcements."

"Okay, then let me off. I'll try to stall them somehow while you race off and get Honon. Gas or no gas, I don't think he'll let this girl get thrown to the wolves."

Lee stopped the motorcycle and Peter hopped off. "Are you sure you can hold them back by yourself?" Lee asked.

"No—but I'll have to, won't I? At least I have this." He patted his revolver. "Now get moving."

As Lee took off down the street, Peter wondered whether it was bravery or stupidity that made him act this way. This was how he had gotten himself involved in the whole caravan business to begin with, by going to Kudjo's aid. On the whole he was satisfied with the way that action had turned out—but how long could he keep bucking the odds?

He ran back stealthily in the direction of the mob, wondering how in hell he was going to accomplish anything. Mark Twain had once written that he'd seen a man of moral courage face down a lynch mob; that was all well and good, but Peter doubted he had the force of personality to carry off such a bluff. *Besides,* he thought, *if anyone recognizes me as Peter Stone, they might want to make it a double lynching.*

The mob was a noisy one, and Peter had no problem following it. It led him to a small park which had been partially converted to communal farmland, although there were still a few trees standing. It was to one of these that the men at the front of the mob dragged the screaming woman. While two men held her, a third knotted the rope he was carrying into a noose.

If I'm going to do anything, it better be now, Peter thought. Everyone's eyes were on the scene in the front, making it easier for him to sneak up behind another tree fifty feet away. Bracing his wrist and taking careful aim at the man with the rope, Peter squeezed the trigger.

The man staggered backwards, clutching at his left shoulder, then fell to the ground. Pandemonium ensued. The mob, which had been in total control of the situation a moment ago, was now not so sure of itself. Heads turned quickly, wondering where the shot had come from.

Peter didn't give them much time to think about it. Being unsure of his aim and not wanting to hit the girl, his next shot went just slightly past the head of one of the men holding her. He placed his next shot over the heads of the crowd, but close enough to scare them.

The mob panicked and broke. Events had changed too swiftly for the mass mentality to comprehend, and now they were the victims instead of the oppressors. Men shouted, turned, bumped into one another in their mad scramble to get out of the line of fire. Peter saw his chance and took it.

One of the men holding the girl—the one Peter had just missed—had bolted, but the other held his ground despite the girl's increased struggles. Peter ran through the crowd, which ignored him as its members tried to flee. The man saw him coming and lifted a club to smash his skull. Peter raised his revolver and fired point-blank into the man's face. The features disappeared in a sea of red as the man fell backward.

The girl screamed, and Peter took her hand. "Come on," he said. "We'd better get away from here before they realize there's only one of me and fifty of them, and I have only two bullets left."

The blank look on the girl's face told Peter instantly that she had not understood him. *She doesn't speak English,* he thought with alarm. *And I don't speak Spanish.* Aloud, he said, *"No habla español.* Come." He beckoned with his arm, trying to convey a sense of urgency. "Come, I won't hurt you."

His gentleness calmed her rising hysteria and persuaded her to do as he said. She followed him as he began by walking quickly, then quickened his pace to a trot. She tried to keep up with him but her pregnant condition hampered her speed. He finally had to slow his own rate to stay with her.

They crossed the park/field and ran along a street bordered by small shops. The stores were deserted, the windows dusty. Peter tried several of the doors, but they were all locked. He didn't think to break a window. Instead they just kept running, looking for someplace that would be safe when the mob regained its composure, which Peter was sure it would do.

They came to an intersection and Peter turned them to the right. They had gone half a block when he heard the sound he'd been fearing—a man's voice yelling, "There they go!"

Pulling the girl sideways with him, he slipped into a narrow walkway between two buildings. She ran after him as best she could, but it was clear to Peter that her legs would not be able to withstand much strenuous exercise. Her face already bore a look of fatigue; only the fact that she was running for her life kept her on the move. Peter had to find a hiding place for the two of them soon or she would be lost.

He gave the doors along the alleyway a quick try as they ran past, but it was no good. They came to the end of the alley and, after a fast check to make sure no one was waiting for them, they dashed to the left up the street.

"They went down the alley!" a man shouted. Peter was at a loss as to what to do. The woman, in her condition, could not outrun the mob, which was already gaining. He would have to find someplace for them to hide, and quickly. But where, that was the problem. This street was another row of stores with no further alleys for them to duck into.

In desperation he tried more doors, and at last found one that opened. He and the girl rushed inside, and he closed the door behind him as quietly as he could. The interior of the store was mostly bare; it had been a dry cleaners, but all the clothing had long since been removed, leaving just some machinery and a long mechanized rack behind a front counter. Dust covered the floor and the top of the counter in a uniform layer bespeaking neglect.

They ran to the center of the room and crouched down behind the counter. Outside the store they could hear the beat of footsteps rushing past, still searching for them. Peter looked at his companion. Her breathing was labored and fear was still in her face. She must have been wondering how this nightmare would end. Peter wanted to talk to her, to assure her, to tell her he had friends who would be coming soon to help them; but the language barrier stood in his way. All he could do was pat her hand and smile comfortingly at her. She smiled back, but it was a very nervous smile.

The sounds of the mob died away outside, but still Peter and the girl didn't move from their hiding place. Soon some sets of footsteps returned. The mob knew that they couldn't have run that far without being seen and were now checking the street for possible hiding places. It would only be a matter of time before they checked the door to this shop and found it unlocked. Peter peered towards the rear and saw that the store did have a back door. That might prove useful.

A set of footsteps walked slowly past the front of the store and stopped. Peter and the girl both held their breath. There was silence for a moment, then a small rattle as the man tried the latch. The door squeaked open inwards, and Peter suddenly had a horrifying vision of what the man would be seeing—two distinct sets of footprints in the dust leading directly behind the counter.

"Hey, they're in here!" the man called to his friends as Peter stood up and aimed his gun. The shot caught the man full in the chest and he fell over backwards, blocking the doorway.

Lifting the girl to her feet Peter pulled her with him to the rear of the store. The door was bolted and the bolt had rusted in its slot; it took him several seconds to force it open. They rushed out the back door and found themselves in the alley they had run through a short while earlier. Going back the way they'd originally come, the two fugitives began running once more.

They made it to the park before the mob caught sight of them again. The crowd of angry men was two hundred yards away and closing the gap rapidly. The girl stumbled, fell and could not get up again. She lay there panting for breath and crying. Peter stood over her, feeling like Davy Crockett at the Alamo with Santa Ana's men coming over the walls. Fortunately, none of the men in the mob was armed with more than a stone or club. *Which means they'll kill me slowly and messily, rather than cleanly with a bullet through the brain,* Peter thought bitterly.

He fired his last bullet into the group and a man fell. Bunched together as they were he could hardly avoid hitting someone. The shot slowed them down and they approached more cautiously. He could see

147

some of them obviously making mental calculations of how many bullets he had fired and how many shots might be left. Even if he'd had more bullets with him, Peter would not have dared stop to reload—the mob would be on top of him before he could finish. He held the gun pointed at the group, trying to look as confident as if it were fully loaded.

The crowd had drawn to within fifty feet when the noise of squealing tires rang through the air. Around the corner came the second armored truck, ready for business. Lee was in the driver's seat, with Kudjo leaning out the window and carrying a machine gun. He intentionally fired a staccato burst directly above people's heads as Lee drove the vehicle off the street onto the ground of the field/park.

With the truck bearing straight down on it, the crowd scattered quickly. One man who wasn't fast enough got knocked to the ground as the armored vehicle brushed past him, but the rest of the mob made it to safety. The truck pulled up alongside Peter and the recumbent form of the girl. " 'Scuse me if I don't look like no white knight," Kudjo said, "but your steed has arrived. Let us away."

Peter helped the girl up gently and into the truck. "Where's the rest of the caravan?" he asked.

"They're going to meet us a little ways south of town," Lee said. "All things considered, Honon decided to go to El Paso for gas, after all."

CHAPTER 10

Five bombs went off at or near banks in Manhattan early Saturday in what a Puerto Rican nationalist group called an offensive against "yanki monopoly capitalism."

No one was killed or injured by the blasts, four of which were in and around Rockefeller Center and the other in the Wall Street area. . . .

The group taking responsibility for the explosions said it was supporting not only Puerto Rican independence but also third-world liberation and freedom for the five Puerto Ricans in jail for the 1950 assassination attempt on President Harry S. Truman and the 1954 shooting of U.S. congressmen on the House floor.

—*Los Angeles Times*
Sunday, October 27, 1974

Like rats trapped in an overcrowded cage, we will find ourselves reacting more and more violently to the situations that oppress us. We are pressed together too tightly for sanity to prevail, yet not tightly enough to solve the problem of a breakdown in distribution. Conflicts are bound to result.

Minor problems become major ones. Major problems become confrontations. Confrontations become wars. . . .

Urban guerrilla warfare can only increase. As the shortages grow and frustrations mount, people will have no outlet for their conflicting emotions except violence. Prejudices and hatred, even long-dead ones, will flare anew as people look for definite scapegoats to blame. . . .

Marx and Engels foresaw warfare between the haves and have-nots, but they thought it would come about because of capitalistic oppression—not because of capitalistic lack of foresight. In fact, in that regard the Communists have been just as lax as we have. . . .

—Peter Stone
World Collapse

*   *   *

Lee spoke a little Spanish, enough to determine that the girl's name was Ninita Hernandez and that she was nineteen years old. He was able to assure her, in halting words, that she was now safe and among friends, and that they would take her to a peaceful place. Still she was inclined to be nervous among these strangers, and Peter had to hold her for comfort.

They rejoined the caravan a few miles southeast of Las Cruces on Interstate 10. Honon, whose Spanish was fluent, interrogated the girl at length. At one point she burst out sobbing and he had to be at his soothing, diplomatic best. Finally he asked Sarah to take her off and examine her, explaining to Ninita that Sarah was a doctor. Then he called Jason and Peter over to him.

"I trust you speak some Spanish," Honon said to Jason.

"It's hard to be a priest in California without learning some of it, if only in self-defense. Even though I was mainly concerned with astronomy, I still had my sacred duties to perform."

"Good, because that girl is going to need your services as soon as Sarah's through with her. She's been through a rough time. Racial tensions were high in Las Cruces; the Latins claimed that the Anglos were monopolizing all the best supplies and the Anglos called the Latins thieves and blamed them for the high population. Ninita's pregnancy was the match that set off the bonfire. This lynching attempt was only the tail end of the matter; she's had more men fighting over her than any woman since Helen of Troy. At the end, a mob of people burst into her house, murdered her husband right before her eyes and started dragging her off to be hung. That was when Peter stepped in to save the day."

Peter blushed at the praise. "She and I would both have been dead if it wasn't for Lee and Kudjo."

"Of course, but the initiative was still yours."

"We will be taking her along with us, won't we?" Jason asked. "It might help if I could give her that much encouragement."

"Of course. Her pregnancy will be an asset at the Monastery instead of a liability. We'll always need kids there."

After the doctor and the priest had done their jobs and pronounced her fit, the caravan started off again to the south, even though it was still daylight. They crossed the border into Texas and were almost to El Paso when one of the cars called in via walkie-talkie to say that it was about to run out of gas. "Well, this is as good a place as any to stop for the night," Honon said, pulling the truck off to the side of the road.

"Are we going to have to abandon that car?" Peter wondered.

"I don't think so. I've got some large reserve cans of gas in the back here; they should be enough to get us into El Paso. But I'd like to get there in the daytime, so tomorrow morning will be all right. We can sleep tonight, for a change."

But the evening did not start out as peacefully as Honon had hoped. Zhepanin had spent the day brooding and refining his theories about Honon's true intentions, and was quite vocal about his beliefs at dinner. "We are nothing but a roving band of outlaws," he proclaimed. "We travel around the countryside robbing and killing at the whim of our leader, who has assembled us solely to support his own ego. We are supposed to be going somewhere, to a mysterious colony and an even more mysterious starship, yet he tells us nothing but fairy tales about them. He does not tell us where they are or who is behind them; is it because he *cannot?* Because such things don't exist except in his imagination? He tells us he wants us to help save Civilization, yet everything we do along the way is accomplishing the exact opposite purpose. Every time we rob, every time we kill, we are destroying what is civilized within ourselves."

"I've said it before," Honon interrupted. "Civilized behavior only works when you're dealing with other civilized beings. The areas we pass through have dropped everything but an eggshell-thin covering of civilization. To survive among barbarians, you must be barbaric. I contend that we are still civilized people, forced into uncivilized situations."

"How can we be civilized if we do such things?"

"Because we remain true to ourselves. If I were to pick up, say, Marcia, and carry her off to the bushes and rape her, *that* would be uncivilized because it would be violating the rules of our own civilized circle."

"Hey, don't knock it," said Marcia. "It's the best offer I've had all day."

The group laughed, and Honon shot the girl a silencing glance. "The point is," he went on, "that if you behave in a civilized manner among uncivilized people, you will very quickly end up robbed, beaten and/or dead."

"One must make a start somewhere."

"Fine. You can do that if you want—but I won't let you risk my caravan in the process."

"That is always the choice you give us," Zhepanin complained. "If we do not like it we can leave. You know full well there is nowhere else we can go, now that we are so far from our homes and friends."

"Would you care to put it to a vote then? That's the civilized thing to do."

The Russian snorted. "I have seen your votes. The

others are all frightened of you and will vote your way, just as in Russia."

"Then what do you suggest?"

Zhepanin looked around, licking his lips nervously. "I would challenge you for the leadership of the caravan."

"A fight? How terribly uncivilized!"

"Do not make fun of me. I am serious."

"Yes, I believe you are." Honon looked the man up and down thoughtfully. "You impress me, Gregor; I really didn't think you would quite have the nerve. I outweigh you by thirty pounds, you know."

"Do you accept my challenge?"

"Sure, let's get it over with so we can all get some sleep."

The two men stepped out apart from the group and began circling one another. Zhepanin moved warily, knowing that Honon was both bigger and more skilled than he was. He crouched low, his guard up to defend against any blows.

Suddenly Honon moved. His body became a blur as he closed in on Zhepanin, swung a leg up and kicked the Russian hard in the groin. Zhepanin let out a cry of pain and sagged to his knees, clutching at his genitals. A wave of vomiting overcame him and he rolled to the ground, tossing up the dinner he'd just eaten.

Honon stood over him unsympathetically. "I could have taken you in a fair fight, too, but I'm tired and you're not worth the effort. If you're going to choose an uncivilized method of settling a dispute, you'd better learn to go all the way with it." He looked around at the group. "Kudjo, assign sentry duties for

154

tonight. I'm going to sleep now. Tomorrow we get gas in El Paso."

While Sarah ministered to the beaten Zhepanin, Peter had a talk with Risa. They hadn't said much to one another since their return from Tucson, and Peter wanted to see how she was feeling. To his relief, she showed some signs of snapping out of her depression, being ever so slightly more responsive to questions than she had been before. He kissed her goodnight and, while there was still minimum response, she was not as wooden.

The next morning, Honon awoke as though nothing out of the ordinary had happened the night before. He and Peter walked down to the camper, where they were greeted by a worried Charlie Itsobu. "I had to scrape the barrel to come up with breakfast," the cook said. "I don't know what we'll do about dinner tonight."

"Don't worry," Honon assured him. "By dinnertime there will be plenty of food."

Peter pondered that remark as he ate. Either they were remarkably close to the Monastery or else Honon was going to get food for them. Perhaps he had a cache hidden somewhere nearby, or perhaps he intended them to steal their food—though this area looked like pretty poor pickings. Personally, Peter found himself favoring the first hypothesis, that they were about to end their journey. The thought excited him.

With breakfast over, Honon brought out the large cans of gasoline he had been holding in reserve in the back of the first armored truck. The car that had run out of gas yesterday was the first priority, after which the remaining reserves were divided evenly among the other vehicles. Within half an hour the caravan was moving again.

Interstate 10 took them right into El Paso. Honon apparently knew his way around here, for he guided the caravan through the city streets with the ease of a native. Around them, El Paso brooded. This was not the silence of a ghost town, such as Peter had seen in Tucson; people were very much in evidence, tending their gardens and gaping at the caravan as it passed. Rather, this was a stillness of expectancy; the city was holding its breath, waiting for some significant event to begin. Peter had the feeling that the waiting would not be long, and hoped the caravan would be refueled and out of town by then.

Honon led them directly up to a filling station. This one, like most of the other operative ones they'd seen, was surrounded by a fence and had several guards patrolling the perimeter. Unlike the previous times, however, Honon showed no trepidation about approaching it in daylight. One of the guards came up to the truck; Honon showed him a card and the guard motioned to one of his companions manning the gate. The fence parted to let them through, and Honon drove his armored truck right up to the gas pump. "Fill 'er up," he said, adding to Peter, "It gives me such a feeling of power to be able to say that."

"It's ten bucks a gallon," the attendant informed him.

Honon didn't even blink. "Oh? Do you give trading stamps?" When the guard failed to react, Honon flashed a wad of bills at him. "Don't worry, we can

156

pay for it." The man, however, insisted on counting out the money before filling the tank.

To Peter, this was just one more piece of evidence that they must be nearing the Monastery itself. Honon had shown no reluctance before to rob gas stations, yet here he paid cash. He would not want to acquire a reputation for dishonesty near his home territory, because he obviously did repeat business here.

But if the Monastery were somewhere nearby, where could it be? Certainly not in the city of El Paso itself; anyone with the foresight to begin such a project would have the foresight to know that a big city was not the place for it—the difficulty of getting food would be monumental in itself, not to mention scores of other problems. The Monastery would have to be somewhere in the country around the city, but Peter was not familiar with the area and couldn't even begin to make a guess. Across the border in Mexico, perhaps?

It took better than half an hour to fill all eight cars, as the attendant made Honon pay for each tank as it was filled. Honon parted with his ill-gotten money cheerfully; he seemed in an exceptionally jovial mood. Finally all the vehicles were fueled once more and, bidding farewell to the taciturn guards, Honon gave the order to move out.

The mood of the city had darkened still further, as though thunderclouds were gathering for an emotional storm. The caravan crawled timidly through the streets like mice hoping to get out of the kitchen without attracting the cat's attention. The feeling of impending disaster was so intense that Peter began to get a headache.

Then the bubble burst. From a couple of blocks to the south, the sound of an explosion ripped through the quiet air, followed closely by the continuing noise of gunfire. The shooting was loud and getting louder, which meant they were approaching the scene of a battle. Honon spent a second listening to the commotion and gauging its direction, then turned the caravan north along a side street in order to avoid it.

Instead, he drove straight into the middle of a battlefield. Both sides of the street had been lined with garbage cans and piles of trash to serve as barricades for the opposing soldiers. Nothing had been happening for a while, but at the appearance of the caravan both sides began firing at the line of vehicles.

"Let's step on it," Honon said into the walkie-talkie. He set the example by gunning the accelerator and tearing off at top speed down the street. Taking the corner on two wheels he turned right, with the other cars only a short distance behind him.

"What's all this?" Peter wondered.

"The last few times I was through here the people of Juarez—the Mexican town just across the Rio Grande—were making unhappy noises about their status. Juarez has always been a tourist town; with that income gone, they've been trying to come across the border looking for jobs. The Texans have tried to keep them out, but the Mexican-Americans living here—who have never gotten a fair deal from the Anglos—seem to have sided with the invaders. I'd say a full-scale war has erupted, with the Anglos fighting on two fronts."

"It makes Las Cruces look like a tea party."

"You've got the idea."

The street they had turned onto was relatively peaceful—only a couple of shots were fired at them by snipers in upper story windows. But as they turned right onto the next street, they again came to entrenched forces shooting it out between themselves, and again the caravan was caught in the crossfire. The continual *pings* of bullets ricocheting off the armored truck threatened to deafen Peter; he wondered how the people in the cars that weren't armorplated were faring.

His question was answered all too quickly as the fifth car in the line suffered a hit of some sort. It went out of control and skidded, slamming into a lamppost and bouncing partially back into the street. One of its fenders clipped the sixth car, which had swerved to avoid it, knocking that vehicle off to the side. It crashed through the barricade on the west sidewalk, crushing two of the snipers who had been kneeling there.

Honon stopped his own truck and was on the walkie-talkie before the action was even completed. "You people in the damaged cars, get out of there fast and take refuge in some of the others. Better to risk bullets than explosions." Even as he spoke, flames began leaping out of the wreck of the sixth car.

Doors opened in the burning vehicle. Gina Gianelli and two of her children—Sophia and Paolo—raced out and were picked up by what had been the seventh car in the line, driven by Jason. Her other three children were safe in the VW van. Dom Gianelli, who had been driving the sixth car, did not move; Peter could see his body slumped over the steering wheel. Peter started to open his own door to go out and rescue him when the car exploded in a ball of flame. He had to shield his eyes from the blinding glare.

"Damn!" Honon whispered between clenched teeth. His hands gripped the steering wheel tightly. "He was a good man. Damn, damn, damn, damn, damn!"

Meanwhile, Harvey and Willa Parks and their two children, Barbara and Joseph, emerged safely from the damaged fifth car. They ran, amid a hail of bullets, toward the Volkswagen van that had been preceding them. Sarah, who'd been driving it, had the side door opened and ready for them. Suddenly Willa fell as a bullet hit her in the left shoulder. Harvey cried out in anguish as he saw her drop, and the children stopped running momentarily; then Harvey shooed the kids in the direction of the van while he went back to pick up his wife. With her in his arms, he raced over and got into the van.

"Okay, everybody," Honon said over the walkie-talkie, "let's try it again, shall we?" His voice was measured, concealing the grief Peter knew he felt at Dom's loss.

The shortened procession took off once more. They turned left at the corner and then left again, leaving a lot of the fighting behind them. They were starting to breathe a little easier when a building on their left suddenly exploded and came crashing down into their path. Honon slammed on the brakes as tons of brick and broken glass smashed on the ground in front of them. His reflexes were slightly faster than Lee's; the second armored truck came screeching to a halt and bumped them roughly from behind. Fortunately, neither of the armored trucks was seriously damaged in the collision, but the road ahead of them was blocked by the debris of the fallen building. "Okay," Honon said over the walkie-talkie, "we turn around and try some other way out of this maze."

Making a U-turn across the broad, deserted street, the caravan started back in the direction it had come. It turned east and then northward again a couple of streets over.

There were the same barricades along the sidewalks, but they appeared empty. As the cars were halfway down the street, however, a group of men armed with automatic weapons stepped out into their path. They formed a semicircle, defying the caravan to continue forward.

"What do we do now?" Peter asked.

Honon put his foot on the brake gently and the lead truck began to slow. The soldiers outside relaxed slightly. "I'll tell you what we're *not* going to do," Honon said, "and that's let ourselves get taken prisoner."

His foot left the brake and smashed the gas pedal hard to the floor. In response, the armored truck shot forward with a drunken leap that caught the men in the street off guard. The ones directly in front tried to leap out of the way, but were too slow. Peter felt the agonizing *thud, crunch* as the truck hit and ran over two of the enemy. His stomach began turning flip-flops, but he set his jaw and tried to think about what they would have done to him had they been given the chance.

The soldiers who had been off to the side commenced firing at the truck once their initial shock had worn off. The bullets ricocheted as before while the truck sped down the street to safety, followed by its entourage.

Then, unexpectedly, there was a *pop* and Honon was fighting the steering wheel for control. The truck swerved off to the left, approaching the makeshift barricades. Honon let the truck go its own direction, turning the wheel only to coax it at the last second. The truck scraped the sides but avoided a full-scale crash.

"They shot out the left front tire," Honon said disgustedly. He picked up the walkie-talkie and re-layed that news to the rest of the cars. "One thing's sure," he went on. "We can't wait here. We'll try limping along until we can find an alley or something that isn't being used as a battleground. Then I'm going to have to change a flat."

CHAPTER 11

Any author who calls attention to a social problem runs the risk of deepening the already profound pessimism that envelops the techno-societies. Self-indulgent despair is a highly salable literary commodity today. Yet despair is not merely a refuge for irresponsibility; it is unjustified. Most of the problems besieging us, including future shock, stem not from implacable natural forces but from man-made processes that are at least potentially subject to our control.

—Alvin Toffler
Future Shock

The future I foresee is a bleak one, what with its strikes and shortages, its hunger and uncertainties, its violence and hatreds. No prophet from Cassandra onward has enjoyed foretelling bad times, yet we are compelled by some perverse sense of duty to carry the alarm. Though we are dismissed as crackpots or reviled as doomsayers, still we must speak out.

This book is meant to serve as a warning. The

163

trends I have foreseen are not totally unalterable, the future not immutable. I'm not saying it will be easy to change the drift of events—the trends I've described have the ponderous momentum of centuries behind them. Stopping this momentum will be a full-time job. It will require enormous sums of money, gigantic amounts of physical labor, tremendous personal sacrifices and, most important of all, leadership by men of vision.

Excuse me for getting pessimistic again for a moment, but men of vision have been conspicuously absent from positions of leadership for several decades now. . . .

—Peter Stone
World Collapse

*   *   *

The caravan crawled slowly through the streets of El Paso, hobbled by the flat tire of its lead truck. The constant bumping rattled Peter's teeth and he wondered aloud how good this would be for the wheel. "That's the least of my problems," Honon told him. "I've got a spare tire in the back. But I'm sure as hell not going to stop right here and get out to fix it."

They managed to find a peaceful street that paralleled the Rio Grande. The river was choked with dead bodies, Mexican and Texan alike; the invasion from Juarez had taken its toll. Peter hoped the bodies would be removed quickly; if they were left to rot the city would have an epidemic on its hands, as germs in the decaying flesh polluted the water.

An alleyway finally presented itself and the caravan turned into it. "Okay, everybody out for a rest stop," Honon announced over the walkie-talkie as he shut off his engine. Following his own advice, he swung open his door and jumped down to the ground to inspect the damaged tire.

Most of the people getting out of the cars appeared shell-shocked to some degree. Gina Gianelli was weeping openly over the loss of her husband as Jason held her in his arms and did what he could to comfort her. Risa and Marcia tried to hide the grief they themselves felt as they alternated tending to the five Gianelli children. Peter went over to the VW van to see how matters were progressing in there.

Sarah was hunched over the supine form of Willa Parks while Harvey and the two kids looked on anxiously. "How is she?" Peter asked.

Sarah didn't bother looking up. "The bullet went clean through her left shoulder. How it missed her lungs I'll never know, but I'm profoundly grateful. There's probably some bone damage. Damn, but I wish I had an X-ray machine handy."

Harvey and the children were in so close that they were constantly jostling the doctor. Peter decided to clear them out so Sarah would have room to work. Taking a tone of command that was unfamiliar to him, he ordered the Parkses out of the van until they were ready to start up again. Reluctantly, they obeyed.

Peter wandered along the row, checking on how people were. Lee and Kudjo had taken machine guns and were guarding the entrance to the alley. That struck Peter as an eminently practical idea, and he sent Charlie Itsobu and the still-healing Bill Lavochek to guard the front end. Helen Itsobu had taken her daughter Machi, who was on the verge of tears, over to the Gianelli children so that the youngsters could cling to one another for security.

Peter went over to where Jason was comforting Dom's widow. He put a sympathetic hand on Gina's shoulder, but she was so deep in her own grief she failed to notice it. Jason looked at him. "I think I can handle her," he said softly. Peter nodded and moved on.

Patty Lavochek and Ninita Hernandez were standing idly by the last car, looking confused and helpless. "Everything all right back here?" Peter asked Patty.

"I guess so, except for that Russian. He was sitting in the back seat while I drove and he was cursing and blaming Honon for this whole mess. He finally lapsed into Russian, but I don't suppose he was saying anything complimentary."

"I wouldn't think so, not after the fight last night. Nobody likes being humiliated and hurt like that. By the way, where is he?"

"I don't know; I thought I saw him go up towards the front when we all got out of the cars. Personally, I was glad to be away from him for awhile; he was getting on my nerves."

Ninita, who had been looking up to the front, suddenly screamed. Peter whirled quickly, not knowing what to expect but trying to be ready for anything.

Honon was kneeling on the ground. He had jacked up the armored truck and had his back outward, removing the old tire. Zhepanin stood behind him, right arm upraised. The crowbar that Honon had used as the jackhandle was in the Russian's fist. There was no question of the engineer's motives—he was going to avenge his defeat the night before by killing Honon.

Ninita's scream caused Honon to turn around just as the crowbar began to descend. The big man's reflexes brought his arm up to deflect the blow even before he consciously realized what was happening. The crack of the crowbar against Honon's right forearm resounded up and down the alley.

In a blind rage, Honon got to his feet, his bearlike body towering over the now-frightened Zhepanin. With his good left hand, the caravan leader yanked the crowbar from the other's grasp, lifted it into the air and brought it down full strength on the back of the Russian's skull. Another crack of crunching bone split the air.

Peter was running down the line of cars, but was too late to prevent Honon from hitting Zhepanin. The big man stood over his would-be killer, prepared to strike more blows, but Peter stepped in and stayed his hand. "There's no point," he said.

The look of maniacal anger faded abruptly from Honon's face. The crowbar clattered to the ground as he dropped it and clutched at his right arm. "Damn, that was all I needed."

Sarah pushed her way through the crowd that had gathered. "Are you people making more work for me? What happened?"

"I think he broke my arm," Honon said.

"Not you, you big lug," she said, kneeling at the Russian's side. "You'd survive a direct nuclear attack. What'd you do to him?"

"Hit him with a crowbar."

Sarah muttered something and began working on

Zhepanin. Honon turned to Peter. "Let that be a lesson to you: never lose your temper," he said. "I may have just cost us a nuclear propulsion engineer we badly need."

Sarah stood up, still looking down at her patient. "If you don't get one end of him, you get the other. Fractured skull, I'd say. It's hard to tell how far the damage extends."

"Can you pull him through?" Honon wanted to know.

Sarah began examining the leader's arm. "I don't think so; not unless I can get a lot more sophisticated equipment. Do you want to try breaking into a hospital and hope it hasn't been scavenged? Yep, your arm is definitely broken."

"I already knew that." Honon winced in pain as she deftly felt her way along the bone. "Look, we'll be at the Monastery by nightfall unless some other calamity happens. They've got a small hospital set up there. Will he last until then?"

"I guess he'll have to, won't he? Luckily, you hit the right side of his parietal area, the hardest part of the skull. Do we have time for me to set your arm?"

Honon shook his head. "No, just splint it and sling it. It'll last until we get there. Can he travel?"

Sarah shrugged. "Again, it's a matter of necessity. If he stays here he'll die for sure, so we wouldn't be hurting his chances by taking him with us."

"Good." He turned to Peter. "Do you think you can fix that tire with only my verbal assistance?" Peter nodded. "All right, I'll be right with you. I just have to make a general announcement."

Turning, he faced the people he had led down

California and across the southern desert for the past couple of weeks. "I've got some news for you all," he said. "We'll be at the Monastery by sundown tonight." A small cheer arose, which he quickly squelched; there was no point to giving their position away to any enemies lurking nearby. "All we have to do," he continued, "is change this tire and we'll be on our way. But it's going to be crowded, since we have to abandon everything but the two armored trucks."

There was general puzzlement over this. "Why?" Jason asked.

"As we are right now, there are six cars lined up like ducks in a shooting gallery. Four of them are totally unprotected. It's a wonder we haven't sustained more casualties than we have, the way the war is going out there. With everybody crowded into the two trucks there will be a lot less target to shoot at—and what target there is will be armored, unless some lucky shot hits a tire again."

"But can we all fit into the two trucks?" Charlie Itsobu asked.

"Well, let's see, there are," he made a quick count, "twenty-five of us still alive. Two are seriously injured and will have to be kept lying down. There are eight children—they'll take up somewhat less room. Two people can ride in the front of each truck. Let's see, why don't we arrange to have Sarah and her two patients in the back of the second truck along with six other adults. That leaves four adults and eight children in the back of this first truck. It'll be cramped, I know, and most of you will have to stand for a couple of hours, but I think we can manage. Why don't a couple of you get busy while Peter is changing the tire and empty out the backs of the trucks? Strip them to the walls; we'll need all the space we can get."

"Even the guns and the motorcycles?" Lee asked.

Honon nodded. "Everything goes. We'll keep a couple of weapons in the cabs in case we run into real trouble, but for the most part we're going to be running. If the people who find this alley after we leave want to use our leftovers to blow themselves up, that's their business."

"What about our personal things?" asked Helen Itsobu.

"If you've got room for them in your pockets, fine. Otherwise, junk them—your lives are more important."

As Sarah put a splint on his right arm and tied it in a sling, Honon supervised the work. Peter was able to change the tire without assistance, and afterwards helped other caravan members empty out the weapons from the back of the lead truck.

"Kudjo and I won't be able to do any driving," Honon said, "so I'll leave that to you and Lee. You and I will take the lead, and I'll give you the directions. All you have to do is make sure that we stay in one piece until we get there."

Peter nodded. That in itself was a tall order, but he did not shrink from the responsibility. He helped the people, particularly the children, into the back of the truck, trying to give each of them a smile or word of encouragement. By the time the last one got in, he was almost ready to believe that encouragement himself. With a sigh, he climbed into the cab and plopped into the driver's seat. "Okay," he said to Honon, "where to?"

"Straight ahead out of the alley and then right for starters. And don't spare the horses."

Peter accelerated slowly to the end of the alley so as not to knock over the passengers in the rear. The street looked peaceful and deserted, belying the fact that there was a war going on. Only the nearby sound of explosions spoiled the serenity.

The route Honon charted for them paralleled the border river. There were fewer bodies in the water along this stretch, but Peter had little time for sightseeing; he had to keep his eyes on the street ahead, always wary of an ambush or some other unexpected development.

"Uh oh," commented Honon, who had been watching the action on the other side of the Rio Grande. "They're bringing in the big stuff, now—mortars."

Peter risked a glance to his right. As Honon had said, the Mexicans were rolling in pieces of field artillery, which they had probably liberated from one of their own army bases. They were being deadly serious in their attempt to get across the river to the "Promised Land," which they were willing to destroy in the process.

"Don't worry," Honon said, "I think they've got better targets to aim those things at than us." Nevertheless, Peter pressed his foot a little harder to the floor.

There was a dull roar from across the way as a mortar was fired. The shot flew well over their heads and exploded several streets off to their left. More shots were fired, and there were more explosions within the city. To Peter, each shot was another wound to the urbanized way of life—a beast that already lay dying. The death throes sent an eerie chill down his spine.

Honon was directing him off a straight route now, turning left and right seemingly at random. Peter checked the speedometer and saw that he was going near sixty even in the downtown area; he was thankful he didn't have to worry about other traffic as he tore through intersections and made turns at these speeds. He took corners by cutting across the curb —a bumpy procedure, but it saved on time.

A roadblock suddenly appeared on the street in front of them. It was not as substantial as the rows of cars that had blocked the highway west of Tucson —just old barrels, boards and trashcans—but it was backed up by a group of very angry-looking men with guns. Peter looked to Honon for instructions.

"Ram it," the big man said succinctly.

Peter steeled himself for the effort and obeyed. His speed shot up to seventy-five as he bore down on the barrier. The men behind the barricade scattered, except for one brave individual who stood his ground, picked up his shotgun and fired point-blank into the windshield of the armored truck. The glass shattered, but held together—and in another moment, the truck was through the barricade and over the now lifeless body of the brave defender.

Visibility was difficult through the shattered windshield, but Peter managed to see by squinting and picking the proper spot. The streets they found now all seemed peaceful; apparently that roadblock marked the current limits of disputed territory. They met with no further incidents and, after awhile, Honon radioed back to Lee to slacken speed—it was clear sailing ahead.

Leaving the dying city of El Paso behind them, they entered country that looked as though it had never even been born. Interstate 10 had been abandoned somewhere in the mess of the city, and now they found themselves cruising along U.S. Highways 62 and 180. The road ran eastward endlessly through empty, dusty terrain. Some scraggly clumps of brush and an occasional hill were the only break in the monotony of the panorama. *This land has never been alive,* Peter thought as he drove. *What a place for the resurrection of Civilization.* He looked questioningly at Honon, who seemed to be in fine spirits. "Just a couple more hours," he beamed at Peter.

About two hours outside of El Paso the road curved toward the north. Faded mileage signs stood beside the highway, telling the distances to Hobbs, Artesia and. . . .

"Carlsbad!" Peter exclaimed suddenly. "Carlsbad Caverns! Of course—what better place for an underground settlement than underground? I'm right, aren't I?"

"I was wondering how long it would take you to figure it out," Honon said quietly. "Carlsbad is one of the most perfect sites in the world for what we wanted. Being underground, it's out of sight of casual passersby, yet it's already hollowed out so we didn't have to pay for excavation work. The caverns are huge and there's lots of them, easily capable of supporting several thousand people. There's plenty of water all through the caverns— that's how they were formed, after all—and we discovered a large subterranean lake to use as an independent water supply. The caverns already had their own power and lighting system, which we made over and adapted. And the main entrance is small enough to be easily defended in case someone chooses to invade us. The place has so many advantages it could have been made expressly for this purpose. You'll see it all when we get there—shouldn't be more than another hour or so." As he talked, he got more and more excited, like a boy awaiting the opening of presents on Christmas morning.

As they crossed back into New Mexico, the tenor of the surrounding countryside became less desolate, more receptive to life. Peter spotted flocks of sheep grazing peacefully on the scrub brush. "A number of Indians are members of our colony," Honon said. "They contribute weaving, agriculture and animal raising. We don't have terribly much red meat—though more than the average person these days, I suspect—but what we do have comes from their flocks, plus a little trading with cattle raisers to the north. Mostly we get by on poultry and rabbits."

Peter couldn't help but feel a tingle of excitement as Honon talked about the Monastery. It was real, after all; it wouldn't fade away like some idle dream. Though he had always publicly supported Honon, a part of his mind had joined Zhepanin in doubting this stroke of good fortune. Having that doubt dissolve was like bathing in whipped cream, a sensual experience of the mind.

"But why did we have to detour through El Paso?" he asked. "Wouldn't it have been simpler just to cut straight across the southern portion of New Mexico to get to Carlsbad from Las Cruces?"

Honon shook his head. "No roads—or at least, none I'd trust. If we'd all been in jeeps I might have tried it, but I didn't want to risk those ordinary cars out here in land like this."

The terrain became more hilly and the signs heralding Carlsbad Caverns became more frequent. Finally they came to Whites City—which was little more than an excuse for some deserted motels—and turned left onto State Route 7. This was a narrow, twisting road that wound among the hills for seven miles. Just when Peter was thinking the curves would go on forever, the road ended at a large, empty parking lot in front of a visitor center. "Don't you use any other cars?" Peter asked, gazing around the empty ground.

"Of course, but we keep them hidden when not in use. Wouldn't do to call attention to ourselves, would it? And speaking of our defenses, were you aware that our trucks have been under observation since before Whites City?"

"No," Peter said, genuinely surprised.

"It's true. Those 'deserted motels' are one checkpoint—and these gentlemen are going to check us out still further.

The men to whom he referred were approaching from the visitor center, carrying rifles that were trained directly on the parked trucks. There were five of them, casually dressed but earnest in appearance, and Peter was willing to bet there were a lot more of them still in hiding with weapons heavier than rifles.

"Don't they recognize their own trucks?"

"Of course they do—but they might have been stolen out from under me, and Kudjo and I could have been forced under torture to tell the Monastery's location. Farfetched, I'll admit, but it pays to be a little paranoid these days. Things are saner once you get inside the Defense Corps ring."

They waited patiently in the cab for the men to approach. When the defenders were within earshot, one of them yelled, "Who is it?"

"It's me, Frank—Honon, Code Number 741-765. I've got some people in the second truck who need immediate medical attention. Come to think of it, I could use a little, myself."

The guard relaxed and lowered his rifle, motioning for the others to do the same. "You're late," he said. "We were expecting you a couple days ago."

"Things happened," Honon shrugged.

"Yeah," the guard smiled back at him. "They have a habit of doing that. Okay, I guess it's all right to unload."

Peter opened the door and jumped down onto the soil of his new home. It felt good under his feet. Going to the back of the truck, he opened the door and called, "Everybody out—we're home."

CHAPTER 12

The environmentalists are fond of using the eloquent metaphor of spaceship earth but this is not the most important point to make about the way in which living things have managed to survive for 3,000 million years and, so far, to evolve. Although everybody seems prepared now to accept that other planets elsewhere in the galaxy are likely to have living beings on them, nobody makes light of the evolutionary barriers which the human race has had to surmount. After two million years of near extinction, is it any wonder that instinct should lead to temporary overfecundity? The truth is that the technology of survival has been more successful than could have been imagined in any previous century. It will be of immense importance to discover, in due course, the next important threat to survival, but the short list of doomsday talked of in the past few years contains nothing but paper tigers. Yet in the metaphor of spaceship earth, mere housekeeping needs courage. The most serious worry about the doomsday syndrome is that it will undermine our spirit.

—John Maddox
—*The Doomsday Syndrome*

I'd like to conclude this book with a word about hope—a commodity I haven't mentioned too often. Hope is an indispensable ingredient of the human condition, the dream that someday, somehow, things will be better than they now are. Some prefer to call it faith, others optimism; I call it hope. . . .

Everything I've predicted would lead us to think our hopes are pretty slender. All the trends point that way. But what's the use of going to bed at night if there's no reason to wake up in the morning? . . .

I mentioned earlier that this book is meant to serve warning, but that's only half true. A warning is no good, no matter how many people hear it, if no one is stirred to action. I've made a number of suggestions that are bound to be unpopular. So be it. We're all angry, or should be, about the condition of the world. But are you angry enough to take constructive action to set things right?

I hope you are—because in that hope of mine is the only hope for the world.

—Peter Stone
World Collapse

*　　　*　　　*

The guards got stretchers to carry Sarah's two patients into the Monastery. The rest of the caravan members stood around the trucks in a disorganized clump, not daring to believe their nightmarish jour-

178

ney was at an end. Peter could feel the tension building to a hysterical intensity until Honon lanced it with, "Why are we all standing around out here when we could go inside and have a bath?"

Baths had been a standing joke all during the trip. Nobody in the party had had one for weeks at the latest, and the only clothes they had were the ones on their backs. The overpowering smell of sweat had become so familiar that it was taken for granted, and it was considered a point of courtesy not to mention it—but everyone in the group had been secretly dreaming of the time when they could bathe and rid themselves of the sour odors.

"Actually," Honon told Peter privately as they walked to the visitor center, "it's a requirement that all newcomers bathe before going into the caves. We don't want any lice getting in, and we have to watch the odor build-up. But making it sound like a luxury makes everyone that much more eager to get to it."

Two communal baths, one for each sex, had been installed inside the visitor center. Honon and Kudjo bid the group a temporary farewell there, they had to get down to the infirmary themselves to have their wounds tended to. "Don't worry," Honon told them, "someone will be coming around to take you to dinner and temporary quarters for the night. I'll see you all in the morning."

The men's bath was actually a metal swimming pool ten feet in diameter. It was unheated, which caused mild consternation at first, but once they got used to it they found it quite invigorating. Soon —except for Harvey and Joseph Parks, who were understandably worried about Willa's fate—they were all laughing and splashing in the water like children. The real world was all but forgotten; this was play-time, and they enjoyed every second of it.

After they'd had half an hour of boisterous activity their guide—a solemn-looking black youth named Russell Hart—came to tell them it was time to eat. Their clothes, they were informed, had been taken out and burned; instead, they were given a choice of new ones. The Monastery clothes were woolen and heavy. "The temperature's fifty-six degrees downstairs," Russell explained, "and it's impossible to heat the caverns, so we dress as warmly as we can." They were given new shoes as well, all of which had thick rubber soles.

Once they were dressed, a quick elevator ride took them seven hundred and fifty feet into the earth to the cavern set aside as the cafeteria. The room was well-lit but cold, and they were glad of their new clothing. The walls of the cavern glistened with beautiful rock formations that looked like delicate lace. Despite their hunger, they were properly awed by their surroundings.

Here they were reunited with the women of their party and were fed a hearty lamb stew. Other inhabitants of the Monastery were also eating here. They seemed a congenial group, talking and laughing, but the caravan members kept to themselves for the moment, still hardly daring to believe this.

After dinner they were again segregated by sexes and led to the transient barracks. They would be staying here for a day or two, Russell explained, until they were sorted out and permanent quarters could be assigned to them. The children were escorted to a special creche while the men were led to a long row of cots, which were as promising as featherbeds to people who had spent the last couple of weeks catching catnaps in the seat of a car. Despite their exuberance at having finally arrived in Eden, they fell immediately into the first deep sleep they'd had in ages.

Morning came by proclamation. That was one of the biggest drawbacks to living underground, Russell told them—you didn't have the sun to set your life by. But the colonists had turned that fact into an asset; with artificial lighting required for everything anyhow, work on all projects could go on continuously in four six-hour shifts.

The men dressed in their clean new clothes and went to the cafeteria, where they met the women and children and had breakfast. Eggs were plentiful, they were told, and they ate omelets until they were stuffed.

Russell and a cute girl named Tina Chin announced that they were to be the party's official guides during this first day's tour of the Monastery. Tina, in particular, brought cheering news—Willa Parks was going to be all right. Her arm would heal in a couple of months and she'd be almost as good as new. Zhepanin's fate was still undecided, but the doctors had downgraded his condition from critical to serious.

The tour started out, logically enough, with the living quarters. The larger caverns had been built up into villages of crude wooden huts, hundreds of them crowded together along narrow, meandering streets. The streets wandered haphazardly to skirt the larger stalagmites, which no one had had the heart to break off. None of the huts was very big—little more than a room for sleeping, sitting and talking—but they did afford privacy. "We *are* pressed for space here, so we do the best we can," Tina said. "Meals are eaten in the cafeteria we just left, and we all have our own scheduled mealtimes to avoid confusion. I'm sorry if that sounds regimented; the food is good and there's plenty of it, which is better than people on the Outside have. We have houses instead of dormitories, which would have been easier, because people need some sort of territorial claim to establish a sense of identity. The house you'll be assigned will be yours, and you'll have your own new neighbors to get acquainted with."

"Where did you get the wood to build all these houses?" Bill Lavochek asked. "I know it doesn't grow around here."

"No," Russell agreed, "it was stockpiled by the planners before the Monastery was set up here. A lot of supplies were—and still are—stored in the town of Carlsbad, about twenty miles down the road."

"Didn't this used to be some kind of government park?" asked Marcia Konigsburg. "How did you get it away from them?"

"We took it," explained Tina. "I wasn't here then, of course. It was about four years ago. The people planning this operation had their supplies all ready to go, waiting for the right moment. Finally there came a time—it was the Army riots, you may remember—when the power of the federal government virtually disappeared, and we moved right in without their even knowing. There were a few park rangers guarding the place, but once we explained what we were doing they were only too happy to join us. Some of them are now among our top leaders."

"We've been building for four years and we're still

a long way from finished," Russell picked up from her. "There are still some caves that have never even been explored. Of course, a lot of the work we're doing is just stopgap—most of the people we've got now will be going on the starship—but we want to build some of it to last. Part of our job here is to salvage what we can of Earth as well as to branch out to a new solar system."

As the group was led through the enormous caverns, they were awestruck by the crystaline beauty around them. The floodlights that kept the rooms lit reflected off stalagmites and stalacites, adding to the cavern's grandeur. And the people of the shanty towns all greeted them warmly. Most of them remembered when they themselves had first arrived and gone through the orientation tour; they smiled and did what they could to make the newcomers feel at home.

Next, the group was led down to the main lake, an enormous expanse of crystal-clear water more than one thousand feet below the surface of the Earth. "There's no swimming allowed," Tina said, "but with an air temperature of fifty-six you don't need it; the water's much too cold, anyhow. This is our primary water supply for washing and drinking, and we've recently stocked it with blind cave fish so that it may soon give us food as well. We take great care to see that it remains pollution-free. There are more pools of various sizes in some of the park's other caverns."

She and Russell led the way to another series of smaller caves. "Just because we don't allow swimming in the lake doesn't mean we don't have fun," she went on. "These are our gyms. Basketball is very popular—we have several leagues formed, and the competition is fierce. Tennis, badminton and gymnastics are all big, too. Plus, there's a lot of sedentary activities, like cards, chess and other board games. We have concerts and put on plays, and even have a small newspaper and printing plant—though the number of copies of anything we print is severely limited by our paper supply. We are seriously trying to preserve everything that was good about the old way of life.

"As long as you realize that it's a closed system, and that everything affects everything else," Peter commented. "We lost sight of that before, and look what happened."

Next, the group was taken down to a cavern even lower than the lake. "This is one of the accomplishments we're proudest of," Russell said. "Our nuclear power plant. There was a small generator and electrical system in the caverns before, but nowhere near enough for our needs. Then, too, we didn't want to be dependent on the outside world for our fuel supplies, since they weren't even going to have enough for themselves. So we put in this nuclear reactor—it'll give us all the power we'll use for at least fifty years without needing any more materials."

"What about food?" Charlie Itsobu asked. "Where do you get it?"

Tina fielded that question smoothly. "There's more than fifty caves in this region of the Guadalupe Mountains, of which Carlsbad is only one. Several of the others are being used as our 'farms.' It of course takes a lot of food to feed forty-eight hundred people. Tons of it—mostly grains— were stockpiled before we came here, but we've been doing our best to become self-sufficient. We use hydroponic techniques mostly, though a few experiments are being conducted to see how well this underground soil and artificial light will grow crops. We can even make a passable flour out of soybeans.

"Our meat supply is skimpy. We have some large flocks of sheep that we graze Outside, and we trade with some Indians to the north for beef. We raise rabbits and chickens down here, and we're doing a good job of breeding their numbers up. Also, I hope none of you is squeamish at the thought, but bats are also a staple in our diet. There are caverns up near the top where you can go in the daytime and harvest them like apples, if you just keep an eye out for possible rabid ones. The guano is great for fertilizer, and we're working on tanning and using bat-wing leather."

They traveled to yet another series of caverns; the layout was becoming very confusing to the newcomers, but their guides assured them that they would get used to it soon. These are the libraries," Tina said. "Not nearly as complete as we'd like them to be, but they cover most subjects, both theoretical and practical. A lot of fiction, too. Four or five copies of each book, several on microfilm and at least one printed text on each—after all, you might not have microfilm viewers on Epsilon Eridani."

The group was led into a construction area, where work was performed in an air of quiet pandemonium. "You can tell we're not finished here," Russell said, waving an arm about him to indicate the scene. Workers, male and female, scurried busily past, but not too wrapped up in their jobs to greet the newcomers.

This scene had instant impact on Peter, and made him realize for certain that he was going to like the Monastery. In the cities outside there were still often crowds, but they milled aimlessly, having nothing in particular to do and nowhere special to go. This was the antithesis, a chamber teeming with life, purpose and direction. These were people moving forward. Whether they succeeded or not would only be known in time, but they were *trying*.

"We were saving these for last," Tina said as they entered yet another series of caves. "The nursery and schoolhouse. We have over five hundred children here, ranging in age from newborn babies to fifteen years old, all learning the skills they'll need to grow up in a new world."

The adults from the caravan all glowed as they looked over the children's area. The younger set had large playrooms and were well supervised. The older children were segregated in groups of similar ages, with no more than fifteen students per teacher. It was obvious that every effort was being made to provide for the future of the human race.

"Are there any more questions?" Russell asked as he led the party back to the cafeteria.

"Where's the starship?" asked Patty Lavochek. "Shouldn't it be around someplace?"

"We don't keep it here," Tina smiled. "We don't have the facilities to care for it. It's over across the mountains west of here, at White Sands. We thought Cape Canaveral might be a little far to commute. Don't worry, you'll see it soon enough."

There were other questions, too—where would they live, how soon would they be fitted into the Monastery's routine, what exactly was expected of them. To these, their guides merely said that they would go back to the cafeteria and meet with some administrative personnel to get all the details sorted out.

Jason Tagon fell into step with Peter as they walked back to the dining area. "I've been doing some hard thinking these last few days about what you said to me out in the desert. You may be right. At any rate, I've decided to pray for God's forgiveness and put aside my vows so that I can be of help to the colony. Gina Gianelli has a hollow spot in her life now that Dom's dead, and I would like to fill it. Her children will need a man around while they're growing up, and who knows—I may become a father in fact as well as in title."

"I'm glad you were able to make a decision," Peter said, patting him on the shoulder. "I hope, for your sake and Gina's, you won't regret it."

"There may be moments, but I think I'll manage."

Kudjo and Honon were standing in the corridor outside the cafeteria, waiting for the group to arrive. Everyone clustered around them, wanting to know how they were. Honon assured them that both were doing well and would be out of their casts in several weeks. "It even looks like Gregor may pull through," Honon added. "The doctors are giving him a seventy percent chance now, though there's likely to be some permanent brain damage."

"That gent always did have a hard head," Kudjo muttered.

The caravan members were herded into the cafeteria to await the administration personnel who would take care of finding homes and jobs for them. Peter hung back a moment to speak to Honon and Kudjo privately. "What are you two going to do now?"

"Take a vacation," Kudjo grinned.

"Normally," said Honon, "we'd go right back out on the road to bring in some more people—but we're going to have to wait until we're a little better before we attempt that."

"Fortunately," Kudjo added, "there's a couple other teams doin' the same work."

"There was going to have to be a hiatus, anyhow, while we switch over to a new system. As this last trip showed, cars are too dangerous now; from here on, I want to make the recruiting trips in horse-drawn covered wagons. It's a hell of a lot easier finding grass than gas. That way, too, we can avoid the paved roads and travel across open country, where there'll probably be fewer nasty surprises."

"Don't you ever get to settle down?" Peter asked.

"No, I'm afraid that, like Moses, we guide people to the Promised Land but never get to stay ourselves." His voice was almost wistful for a second, then returned to gruff good humor. "Besides, I'd go crazy in one place, doing one thing. I won't even be going on the starship. This is my world, for all the crazy things it does; I'm happy to go out and explore it and fight it and eventually die in it. It's just my karma, I suppose."

"I'd like to go along with you."

Honon narrowed his eyes slightly and looked Peter over. "Well, I thank you for the offer," he said at last, "but I don't think that's a wise move. You'll be needed too badly here. We've got a lot of honest people who can work with their hands, and we've even got a number of brave souls who can bull their way through dangerous situations. But there's a severe shortage of thinkers, men who can see the future coming and sound the warning. Stay here."

"I guess you're right," Peter sighed. Shaking hands with both men, he went inside the cafeteria.

There were three people from the administration interviewing members of the caravan individually to determine their niche in the new society. It appeared to be a lengthy procedure, and Peter was about to sit down and await his turn when he saw Risa looking at him from across the room. She averted her gaze when he matched it, but he went over to talk to her anyhow. *This is how the whole thing started,* he thought with a wry grin. "How are you feeling?" he asked her.

"Fine." Her eyes were downcast and her voice was muffled, but there seemed to be more life in it than at any time since they'd left Tucson.

"I'd like to speak to you alone for a few minutes."

"Okay."

They left the cafeteria together. Honon and Kudjo had gone, so they were alone in the passageway. "I was watching you as we took the tour this morning," Peter began. "You seemed a lot more like your old self."

"It's all so exciting. The people are doing things and there's hope all around. I guess it's catching.

Peter nodded. "There're new dreams for everybody —including us." He lifted her chin until he was looking squarely into her face. "I meant what I said in Tucson, Risa—I love you.

For the first time in several days he saw her smile. "I . . . I wasn't sure any more. I mean, that was worlds ago, and we were both different people." She paused, considering her words carefully. "Things have changed since then, and I wasn't sure whether you'd regret what you said, or whether you'd just said it to cheer me up. There's a lot more women available now than there were; you could have your pick."

"The one I'd pick would still be you." He pulled her toward him with his left hand while with his right he gently caressed her cheek. "We complement each other, I think. I operate on logic, you on emotion. I've seen too much, you've seen too little. I'm a cynic spiced with idealism, you're an idealist tinged with cynicism. The pieces of my puzzle fit your solution— what more could any couple want?"

He didn't give her much time to answer, though, for his lips were pressed to hers in a long, passionate kiss. She spent a second in a state of uncertainty; then her arms wrapped around him and she returned the kiss with an equal amount of ardor.

Centuries later, it seemed, they separated, looking at each other with a glow in their eyes. Despite the chill in the air, Peter felt decidedly warm. "Shall we go inside and tell the administration people that we'll only need one house between us?"

She smiled and gave him a quick hug.

"And while we're at it," he went on, "we might as well arrange for Jason to perform a ceremony for us."

While they clung to one another Peter glanced around at the beauty of Carlsbad and considered the hope for Mankind that it represented. *Maybe it won't be such a bad world after all,* he thought. And with a satisfied sigh he and Risa went into the cafeteria to rejoin the others.

MORE EXCITING FICTION ON NEXT PAGE!

ROGER ELWOOD talks about

Laser Books

No. 1. Renegades of Time by R. F. Jones
Ray Jones can tell a story as well as any man.
Read this and see what I mean.

No. 2. Herds by Stephen Goldin
Steve Goldin's ability to weave the alien world
into the fabric of our contempory world is
uncanny.

No. 3. Crash Landing On Iduna by Arthur Tofte
Written by an "old pro". As you'd expect, it's
adventure as it should be written with an
ending that will surprise!

No. 4. Gates Of The Universe by Robert Coulson
and Gene DeWeese
This top flight writing team have come up with
a winner. Several of their characterizations are
really outstanding.

No. 5. Walls Within Walls by Arthur Tofte
This is Arthur's second novel in the series. It
has beauty and grace and much human
understanding. A rare combination in a S.F.
adventure. I think you'll agree.

No. 6. Serving In Time by Gordon Eklund
Gordon is really establishing himself in the S.F.
world. With this exciting tale, he gives us a
lesson in history too.

No. 7. Seeklight by K.W. Jeter
As Barry Malzberg says in his introduction, "one
of the three or four best first S.F. novels I have
read."

No. 8. Caravan by Stephen Goldin
As I said about his first novel in our series, "His
ability to weave the alien world into the fabric
of our contempory world is uncanny."

MORE EXCITING TITLES ON NEXT PAGE!

No. 9. **Invasion** by Aaron Wolfe
This is the first novel Aaron Wolfe has ever written. As Barry Malzberg says of it, "It is simply one of the most remarkable first novels, in any field, that I have ever read."

No. 10. **Falling Toward Forever** by Gordon Eklund
This is Gordon's second offering in our series. It's straight S.F. adventure this time, with a deeply human thread, and it's very, very good.

No. 11. **Unto The Last Generation** by Juanita Coulson
Juanita is the wife of Robert Coulson, a co-author of Laser Book No. 4. I think you'll really enjoy her story and that you'll delight in the poetic mood she manages to convey.

No. 12. **The King of Eolim** by Raymond F. Jones
A deeply sensitive story about a family whose son is retarded by their society's standards. At the same time there's lots of excitement and adventure. It takes a Ray Jones to blend these two elements as masterfully as this story does it.

ORDER BOOKS WITH HANDY ORDER FORM BELOW!

To: **LASER READER SERVICE**
M.P.O. Box 788, Niagara Falls, N.Y. 14302
*Cdn. Residents: Send to Stratford, Ont., Canada

Please send me the following books:
☐ #1   ☐ #2   ☐ #3   ☐ #4   ☐ #5   ☐ #6
☐ #7   ☐ #8   ☐ #9   ☐ #10   ☐ #11   ☐ #12

All books are 95c each. To help defray postage and handling cost, please add 25c. I enclose $...... (No C.O.D.'s)

Name ....
Address ....
City/Town ....
State/Prov............. Zip/Postal Code .....

All Fall Down

DATE DUE	BORROWER'S NAME
	~~Daniel~~
	Daniel
	~~Datzia~~

No. 309 Waverly Publishing Co.

DATE DUE	BORROWER'S NAME